little
Green
man
in
Ireland

little green man in Ireland

A Mystery by Mary Branham

SUNSTONE PRESS

SANTA FE

The events, people, and incidents in this story are the sole product of the author's imagination. The story is fictional and any resemblance to individuals living or dead is purely coincidental.

Cover design by

Sunstone books may be purchased for educational, business, or sales promotional use. For information please write: Special Markets Department, Sunstone Press, P.O. Box 2321, Santa Fe, New Mexico 87504-2321.

First Edition

Library of Congress Cataloging in Publication Data:

Branham, Mary, 1929-
    Little green man in Ireland / Mary Branham
        p. cm.
    ISBN: 0-86534-248-2 (hardcover) ISBN: 978-1-63293-110-8 (softcover)
    1. Title
PS3552. R3238L5   1996
813' .54—dc20   96-12084
                                    CIP

Published by SUNSTONE PRESS
            Post Office Box 2321
            Santa Fe, NM 87504-2321 / USA
            (505) 988-4418 / *orders only* (800) 243-5644
            FAX (505) 988-1025

FOREWARNED

On a hot Tuesday morning in late July, the Times announced showers due.

Like most other Londoners who read that the dry spell was ending, Ian Hardwicke related this news directly to himself. Stretching his long, expensively clad legs, he settled into the deep sofa in Sydney Reardon's sitting room and happily thought, "With Sydney's help and a little luck the sale will be consummated by the time flowers bloom, the money will be in a Swiss bank and I'll be on holiday."

"Jesus," Sydney said when she heard rain was predicted, "I've been sweltering here for a month and now that the drought is breaking I'm going to New York. It's hell to be broke." But she had been broke in Paris, and in New York which she still thought of as her hometown, broke once in Budapest and now she was broke in London. For Sydney, broke only meant missing a payment to Cartier's on her emerald ring and flying tourist class.

Kimberleigh Brennan read about rain on the way standing at Heathrow waiting for a bus. Dryness and heat had not depressed her so there was little thought given to showers. She was finally recovering from having her longtime lover, housemate and best friend disappear with his law partner's wife. She had a new hair style, a new Ungaro jacket and was on her way for almost a week with her favorite relative Sydney Reardon, the irrepressible, glamorous cousin of her father's who had been her girlhood idol.

Walter Carrasco read the rain forecast looking out the window of his suite at the Hilton on Park Lane as he waited for a call to go through to his mother. He could tell by the lethargic pace of pedestrians on the sidewalk below that it was still hot. But it would be cool on Carmine Street as his mother sat at her kitchen table, drinking coffee and waiting for the call saying he'd arrived safely. "Your mother's the only woman in the world you give a damn about," Sydney Reardon once teased him. He hoped he'd have time to ring Sydney. It was hard to tell where this assignment would lead. At least he would send her flowers—the florist kind. She was definitely not the type you'd pick blossoms for in the park, no matter how profusely they bloomed. The telephone rang.

Henry James read of the predicted London moisture as he looked out at the slow drizzle falling on Princes Street. Being a native of the West of Ireland he found London a bit hot even in good years. The slow Edinburgh rain satisfied him and he turned back to an article he was trying to finish on Hieronymus Bosch.

Danny O'Rahilly, also called Calcularius, read that flowers would bloom anew as he ate his only real meal of the day in a corner house not far from the late night club in Soho where he had been doing his magic act for the last eight weeks. "Working nights and sleeping days, who gives a shit about flowers?" he thought. The rain might make it cool enough to sleep, though. Next week he'd have his papers and be in New York so what matters the weather.

Statisticians could predict rather accurately from among those millions who read the good news of rain, the number who would die, give birth, win at the races, go on holiday, take bankruptcy, in the week before the grass greened and the flowers bloomed.

But Ian Hardwicke, Sydney Reardon, Kimberleigh Brennan, Walter Carrasco, Henry James and the man called Calcularius could not predict on that hot Tuesday that within that week one would be in the hospital, one would be in love, one would be confused and frightened, one would be facing a long prison term and two would be dead.

1 "Does anyone else get dunning letters from Van Cleef and Cartier's all in the same week?" Sydney Reardon's throaty laugh drifted through the open bedroom door, muffled by the silk shirt she was pulling over her head.

"I don't mind hiding away, up to a point. Especially in London. And there is a certain chic in avoiding the most high-class sort of creditors. But dear heart, I *have* to be back in New York next week. There's a suite of offices I've contracted to pretty up—a publisher—all paneled walls and sporting prints."

She stepped through the doorway, a can of hair spray in one hand, hairbrush in the other.

"I do so hate to be broke in my hometown. When do you think I'll get the go-ahead on Carleton Place?"

Ian Hardwicke forced himself to stop pacing and sank into a chair. He struck a lazy pose and took a sip of the Black Label she had poured for him.

"Be patient, darling. I assure you he wouldn't let another decorator touch that horror house. He's set on you because he adores American girls." He watched her appreciatively. "And besides, you're seeing Agnes Milford-Smythe about her flat. Old Agnes is certain to bribe you with a handsome advance. May I pour you a drink before you dash?

He was hoping to delay her flight. It was important that he talk with her.

"Oh, no. Agnes is one of those health perverts. All yogurt and sparkling spring water. Not a drop of booze in the house. Scotch on my breath would scotch the deal."

Really, Sydney Reardon was too much fun, Ian thought with affection. Her background was impeccable but she never seemed to worry about what she did or what people thought of her. Except when it came to business. If only she had a scholarly knowledge of art, what a setup they'd have together. This made him think of Henry and he sighed. How pedestrian the fellow was, how boring. And now with the new problem this morning, Henry was certain to be timid and tiresome.

He looked about the flat. A soft breeze fanned sheer curtains into the room from open French doors. He walked out onto the balcony and looked down five stories to the traffic moving along Piccadilly. Below, a yellow awning was being cranked out over the third floor terrace. An art show strung along the Green Park fence had enthusiastic tourists bunched beside the paintings.

It was like Sydney to have a sitting room with a balcony when she was terrified of heights. What a contradiction this woman was. Windows wide open summer and winter but usually a fire burned in the hearth, even in July. Her London *pied a terre* was ordinary enough, but conveniently located. "Near theatres and restaurants and not too close to a house of worship," she described it. A residential hotel of some forty-odd rooms and a few suites with a name so tiresome no one could remember it. He glanced at the awning and read upside-down the stenciled name DEVON in bold letters.

"Where do you stay in London?" her New York friends asked.

"Oh, Jesus," was the answer, "a horrible little trap where my grandmother used to stay. I started going there with the family and could never get away." And then she'd laugh and change the subject. That was Sydney, seemingly open and candid, and yet, somehow mysterious. Or did she just value her privacy? When did she ever tell you anything? He really didn't know her very well. And yet, when the telephone call came this morning she was the first person he thought of who could help them and would ask no questions.

It was odd, this feeling that he hardly knew her. He'd actually seen a good deal of her since she was described to him by a mutual acquaintance as the "cleverest decorator I know." That was four years ago. Now she was here more and more of the year and when he was in New York they met for drinks or the theatre. A few times they'd been intimate in a casual sort of way.

Ten or twelve years ago she had been a fairly well-known actress on Broadway. Anyone who read American fashion magazines would remember her tall, model-thin figure, her short, straight dark hair, her wide smile. These days her picture made the Sunday supplements as "the American decorator everyone is talking about."

Ian realized his timing was all wrong. Sydney was distracted and he could hardly hold her attention. Now she was emptying the contents of one handbag into another. For her, noon was far too early for an appointment. In a moment she would be rushing out.

He went across the room and took her arm. "Sit down, old dear, just for a moment. I *must* talk to you."

She looked up, surprised by the urgency in his voice.

The telephone rang.

"Shall I answer?" Ian asked impatiently.

"No thanks, luv, I'll get it, wherever it is." She was searching for the telephone which, as usual, was hidden under a cushion to muffle the sound.

"Hello," she said breathlessly. Sydney always answered the telephone as if she had just come in from some frightfully important and exciting engagement or was just rushing out and had run back just to catch the call. The telephone was on a long cord and might be anywhere in her three rooms and she often had to search for it.

"Kim darling. You're at the airport. Oh luv, I should have met you. I thought it was tomorrow. Come along then."

She covered the mouthpiece with her long fingers. "Kim Brennan, an enchanting child. I thought she was arriving tomorrow." Holding the receiver away from her ear she winked at Ian. Kim's voice filled the room.

"It's fantastic Sydney. I've been moping around, boring everyone. Mum and Dad insisted I go to Italy for a couple of weeks and then come on here. I didn't want to but you know Mum thinks that Italy cures anything, or everything. She was right. Sitting on the steps in front of the Duomo in Florence I suddenly began to feel better and...."

Sydney covered the mouthpiece again shaking her head at Ian and smiling. "Don't give me all the details right now, Kim. Just come along. I'll have a room for you."

"Fascinating conversation that."

"You'll adore Kim. She's the daughter of a cousin of mine but more fun than most relatives."

"She sounds about eighteen and you know I abhor children."

"Heavens—twenty-five or six, at least. I feel she's still a child because when I remember her best she was going to one of those progressive schools that send you off to work every other semester. She wanted to be an actress and I got her on as an apprentice at a summer theatre where I used to play. Quite talented, got a few parts and then, on the spur of the moment, went off with this jock just out of law school. To live in some fashionable pastel town in California where his father had a lucrative law practice.

"Somehow they never got around to marrying but they were together for years. Upset her family. His too, I expect. They seemed very happy. Anyhow, about six months ago he left Kim and his father's practice and went off to Hawaii with the wife of one of the partners in the firm. He and Kim were into swimming and surfing and skiing and tennis. They went to Hawaii and Switzerland and New Zealand but didn't travel this direction, so this is her first time in London."

Sydney was glancing at her diamond watch. "She's glorious looking, all soft and sexy with big, wide grey eyes, something of the ideal American girl of the shampoo ad variety. Her father, Thaddeus Kimberleigh Brennan, is a well-known surgeon down in New Orleans and her mother is a dear—a little earnest but sweet—does good works for fun, that sort of thing. You will probably fall madly in love with her."

"But darling, I'm already in love with you." He flashed his ready smile. "Even if you won't listen to me."

It was almost true, Sydney thought. If Ian were capable of love without financial gain, he might very well love her.

"Dear heart, I must dash. Agnes will be furious if I'm late. Tell you what, come round for drinks later and we'll have a nice long talk."

Ian sighed as he walked to the door. Reluctantly he accepted the invitation.

The double-decker bus with its trailer piled high with luggage seemed an exotic vehicle when Kim boarded it. But after half an hour it was miserably uncomfortable. She stood in the center aisle, unable to move. Clutching a pole, she was stabilized by a portly businessman on one side and a long-haired boy in tight jeans on the other. Seated regally in the back was an Indian family, the mother with red sari and nose diamond, the daughters in pale, fluttering chiffon, all looking so cool, elegant and feminine that she felt a trifle dull in her new jacket even though several men on the bus eyed her. Kim was accustomed to inviting glances from men. She ignored them with that gracious practiced serenity of a girl who never knew an awkward age.

"Miss Reardon is out," the switchboard operator said when Kim rang from the terminal. Interesting, after two marriages Sydney still used her maiden name. Her second husband, Elliott Townsend, was a distinguished theatrical producer some twenty years older. He had died four or five years ago and, in her own words, "too old to be an ingenue and not talented enough to be a leading lady," she had turned to decorating.

Kim gave her name. "Yes, Miss Reardon is expecting you. We have a room waiting."

The lobby was a dim green cave after the brilliance of Piccadilly. Its walls were paneled in dark wood, the tall windows masked with heavy velvet portieres and the carpet a lighter shade of green. The hall porter was green too, in a splendid but slightly shabby uniform which gave an eerie pallor to his face. But he was kind and solicitous.

"Miss Reardon has just come in. You're to go to her directly." He bowed and guided her to the lift.

Sydney flung open the door. "Hello there! Come in." She held Kim at arm's length a moment and then stooped to draw her close in a bear hug. At five-three Kim never felt short except around Sydney who somehow managed to make her five-ten ideal.

"Two years! Is it possible?" Sydney continued hugging her, smiling. Perfect white teeth in a too-big mouth, one of her most appealing features. "I'm glad you're here at last."

"So am I. I've been so hurt and embarrassed and oh, you know, at loose ends. And lonely."

"You won't be lonely here. London is not that kind of town. How's your mother? Fine, no doubt, and still aiding good causes. And how is Tad, that stunning man?"

Kim laughed. "Dad's fine. You never forget a good looking man, even a relative. Who's got the inside track these days?"

"You'll meet him soon, nothing serious but he's divine, sort of Peter O'Toole at his smoothest."

The coffee table was set for tea but a sideboard was filled with at least a dozen bottles and mixers. Sydney poured drinks and started planning Kim's stay in London. "We'll see a play, some new people, some fun. You've been bereft long enough. I have to run over to Dublin the end of the week on business. You'll come along."

"I don't know. I really should go home."

"Nonsense. You'll adore Ireland."

An unctuous, middle-aged waiter came in carrying a tray of tiny sandwiches and cakes. The telephone rang. Sydney answered with her practiced breathless hello, motioning to the coffee table. Kim picked up a sandwich and walked out on the tiny balcony.

"Come back inside," Sydney called anxiously as she put down the receiver.

"You have a marvelous view of the park but that railing is so low you could step right over."

"Maybe you could, dear heart, but I couldn't. You know how I am about high places. I like this room. The view is nice, isn't it, but I never, never step out on that balcony. I keep the doors open whenever the weather is good which, of course, it rarely is."

Kim remembered Sydney's fear of heights. In their house at the beach she used to close her eyes and ask Kim to guide her down the steep circular iron stairs that led to the water. Kim always imagined it was the actress at play.

Sydney changed the subject as she handed Kim a drink.

"Ian's a darling man. He'll be here in a few minutes. Suave, cool, rich. Well, I don't know whether rich—you can never tell about the British. But from an impressive family. Titles, country houses, all that business."

"How did you meet him?"

"Decorated his office. One of the first jobs I had here."

"What kind of an office? What does he do for a living, I mean."

"Oh, you know, import-export," Sydney answered vaguely.

"What does he import? Or export?"

Sydney laughed. "Anything there's a demand for, he always says. Mostly art, I think."

Kim stood up and looked around the room. "Somehow, I can't get used to your living in London. You seem so, so settled here."

"Not settled exactly, but spending more and more time. I lease this funny old place by the year and keep my things here. Actually, I do think of it as home now. The only home I have anymore. Just think, I came here first when I was seven." She took a sip of her drink and looked into the fireplace. "For some reason I'm catching on here. They really like me."

Kim sipped her tall, cool drink. It was like Florence, she no longer felt lost.

"You look marvelous, Sydney."

"The tone of your voice sounded as if you almost added—for your age."

She hadn't thought of age, in fact though she knew Sydney was older and light years away in sophistication and experience, she had never known her age exactly.

"Forty-six last month, luv. Seems old to you at, let's see, twenty-six?"

Kim groaned. "Twenty-eight, in a couple of months."

"How ghastly!"

There was a knock.

"That must be Ian."

The most glorious man Kim had seen off a television screen walked in. He bent and kissed Sydney and then held Kim's hand lingeringly before he settled into a chair.

Kim decided that Ian Hardwicke indeed had a real likeness to Peter O'Toole. He was quite a bit over six feet and very slim, with a bearing that would be military if he were not so relaxed and easy. His hair was light brown with rustles of gold and his eyes were a startling bright blue that made him appear to look through one. His skin was tanned and ruddy. You could imagine him in riding clothes, on a motorcycle, at the wheel of a racing car, on a sailboat. He was probably forty-something, which was an interesting age to Kim. She thought on closer observation that he wasn't really all that handsome but he had the air of someone used to being noticed. Is he married, she wondered immediately. As if it made any difference.

"Scotch of course, luv," Sydney was saying without waiting to pour his drink. Kim noticed that she poured a generous amount, ignoring the ice fast melting in the silver bowl. She wondered if the cubes would last until she had a second drink.

"Do you suppose European ice is different from ours?" she mused and then was uncomfortable when they both turned to look at her. "I mean, the ice melts so much faster. I ask for ice in water and before I've had two sips the ice is completely gone." She felt like a school girl, but Ian was smiling at her.

"Just our poor quality ice, I expect." He dropped a couple of cubes into her glass before she could protest.

"One thing I can never understand," Sydney observed, "is how they keep soda from exploding all over the place. Half the time it's not refrigerated and you see teenagers ordering that vile orange or green carbonated stuff and the clerk just pops off the top. Why doesn't it hit the ceiling?"

Kim smiled gratefully. For all her *savoir faire,* Sydney sounded like an American girl on her first trip abroad.

Ian looked indulgently at both of them, crossing his long, elegant legs and lighting a cigarette. Hiding his impatience with idle chatter, he plotted how he could get a moment alone with Sydney.

Kim was intrigued. He made the usual pleasantries about the weather and her flight from Florence seem important.

"You live in California, Sydney tells me."

"I've been living there but I don't suppose I'll stay on. I haven't really decided where I should live." She sounded so earnest and driven. Suddenly it didn't seem to matter where she lived. The conversation was inane and charming and laughs were frequent.

Ian was asking about their plans for the evening.

"I called for tickets for the revival at the Drury Lane. Kim's first love is the theatre."

"After Scott, of course," she said before she thought. Both Sydney and Ian stared at her. "I mean he used to be my first love." She felt herself blushing.

"Well, yes," Ian said. "An early dinner with me, perhaps? Or a late one?"

"Thanks, no, Ian." Sydney did not confer with her guest. "We'll have a bite here and later, if Kim is not too tired, we'll be reminiscing. I don't want you to know that much about her."

Ian laughed good-naturedly, turning his attention to Kim."How long will you be in London?"

"Two or three days, I expect. Sydney is trying to persuade me to go to Ireland with her at the end of the week and I have to leave for home on Monday."

"On Monday," Ian repeated. "I see."

"I have an excursion ticket and my twenty-one days will be up on Monday." She looked at Sydney. "If I'm going to Ireland, I'll have to change my reservation."

"Not a problem. You can leave from Shannon. We'll rent a car and drive around and then I'll fly from there too." Sydney turned to Ian. "She'll love Ireland won't she? Her great-great-grandmother came from Ireland so they'll love her. It's a dear country, isn't it?"

He was enthusiastic in his praise. "But of course my heritage is Irish on my mother's side. I was at Trinity and have always had a special affection for Dublin." He pondered for a moment and turned to Sydney. "Henry James and I are planning on flying over Sunday for a look at a collection that's to be auctioned at Durrow House. We could go a day early and perhaps have a night on the town, as you Americans say. And I think Kim might enjoy a look at an Irish country house."

"Marvelous," Sydney said at once. "Do you agree?"

"Oh, yes." Kim almost clapped her hands. She surprised herself by agreeing so easily.

"Dublin doesn't swing like London, but I think you'll find it delightful in a different sort of way. Good, it's settled then." He turned to Sydney. "I don't recall, have you met Henry?"

"Your art critic friend? No, I think not."

"I thought perhaps you'd met when you were decorating the office. He's a very old friend. We were at school together. Bright chap, hung up on art—criticism of art, actually. He's teaching now but I'm working on a directorship for him. Private museum. Just the thing. It will give him more freedom for study and writing. You'll like Henry," he said to Kim. "He's coming down from Edinburgh tomorrow."

"From Edinburgh? Is he coming on that exciting train? What's the name? The Scotland Flyer?"

"I think that's a sled, not a train," Sydney laughed.

"I've always wanted to take it. And the Orient Express."

Kim's confusion—and enthusiasm—were refreshing, Ian thought. "The Flying Scotsman, you mean."

"I wasn't far off, was I? Ever since I was a teenager and started reading mysteries. It goes all the way to Istanbul. Do you think anyone was really murdered on those trains?"

"To answer your questions, yes, in point of fact, I expect that someone has been murdered on both trains. But, alas, they are no more, at least not in their original guise as the fastest and most elegant transportation of an era. Actually, Henry's flying in. Why don't we all meet him and have lunch on the way back to town? If we leave the beaten path, as it is called, I know a charming inn."

They thought it a fine idea.

"Splendid. I'll ring you tomorrow morning about time."

Sydney walked with him to the door. "What was it you wanted to ask, luv? We didn't have a chance to really talk."

"Oh, that, it will keep." He smiled at her.

"That's absolutely the most sophisticated man I've ever met," Kim said when Ian was gone. "I felt so *gauche* chattering on and on like a child but somehow he made me uncomfortable, as if I were in the presence of a celebrity. At the same time, he seemed so terribly at ease I should have been too."

"He is sophisticated isn't he, whatever we mean by that term these days. He has that aura of success."

"Did you say he is a lord or something?"

"I didn't say that—he's the younger son—no title himself but from a background full of titles." Sydney returned a seltzer bottle to the sideboard. "I think somehow he minds not having a title. Maybe that accounts for his tremendous energy and drive. He compensates."

"And he isn't married?" Kim asked as she emptied an ash tray into the fireplace.

"Isn't it a miracle? I think it's a case of having too much. Women pursue him so blatantly that he's never had to stop and make up his mind. Or maybe he's just too smart to be caught. I don't know. His older brother is very domestic, he says. Married a county frump and is madly reproducing the family name. Of course, he inherited the title with the lands and all. Perhaps Ian thinks it isn't worth the trouble to marry. That's only my theory," Sydney said as she dried glasses and put them away.

"What do you suppose Henry James will be like? Where did he ever get that name?" Kim laughed. "And he writes too."

2

"Let it ring a bit longer, will you? Thank you."

Henry was probably not three feet from the telephone but he would be reluctant to stop whatever he was doing. Ian Hardwicke was an impatient man and would never have waited for anyone as he so often waited for Henry James unless that man was essential to him. At this time he was essential. It had occurred to Hardwicke that he might be wise to disassociate himself from Henry. The fact that they had known one another since Trinity was not the real reason he kept up the relationship. They had never been friends really, though he had been flattered by Henry's open admiration. At college Henry was interested mostly in art and boxing, and neither of those subjects seemed too absorbing to Ian. Since that time Ian had developed a very real commercial interest in art and Henry was useful when he could verify the authenticity of a painting or a piece of sculpture. Now that he was making a reputation as an art critic it made Ian a trifle nervous. He was beginning to be noticeable.

At last the receiver was lifted.

"Yes?" Henry James' voice had an edge of annoyance and a slight blur of preoccupation.

"Hardwicke here. I thought you'd never answer."

"I'm working on a piece on Bosch. It's due in a fortnight and I can't get it to hang together quite."

"Oh, Bosch," Ian murmured. "Look, leave that for a minute, will you? Something important's come up. I've rung you twice."

"I was at the library. Out most of the day."

"Obviously. A change in plans. We have to make delivery in New York on Tuesday."

"New York. Impossible! They agreed to pick it up in Dublin."

Ian snapped into the telephone, "My dear fellow, for a million pounds nothing is impossible. They've simply balked at coming."

"Well, who do you suggest deliver it? I'm out. We've already discussed any involvement of that sort for me. My reputation as a critic is more important to me than any amount of money."

Ian cut him off with an oath. "*I* made your reputation. Before I took you in hand you were a scholarship boy in dowdy coats and mismatched trousers, giving drawing lessons to young ladies on Saturday afternoons for drink money. So let's not talk about your bloody reputation." After his outburst Ian relaxed a little. "I'd take it over without hesitation but if our buyer identified me, I'd be dead for legitimate business from now on. You talk of your reputation. Consider mine."

"All right. Who's taking it then?"

Ian Hardwicke seldom lost his poise and did not admit to Henry that he too had panicked when the telephone call came this morning. Nor did he tell him of his first plan to ask Sydney Reardon for help. "While you were at the library," he emphasized the word sarcastically, "I evolved a little plot but you have to be here to work it."

"Right now?" Henry groaned "My Hieronymus Bosch...."

"The trouble with you, Henry, is you're always preoccupied with someone like Bosch. If I didn't look after your interests...."

"What's the plot you've evolved?" Henry broke in.

"You remember Sydney Reardon, don't you. Tall, chic, legs a bit too thin, an American? She decorated my office. Frightfully amusing."

"Perhaps. I'm not certain I've met her."

"She has a young relative visiting. Kim Brennan. Perfect for us. Beautiful, too. I'm at the Club now but I've just come round from drinks at Sydney's. My first thought was, God, she's beautiful. Then she chattered on and on, completely ingenuous, and it struck me. She's absolutely perfect. I'll wager she could get by with anything. If she happens to be stopped by customs, she's so...." Ian groped for the proper descriptive word.

"Dumb?" Henry supplied.

"No," Ian said sharply. "Not dumb. She's actually frightfully bright, I think. But so guileless. Yes, that's it, no one would doubt her. Sydney's taking her to Ireland in a day or so and she departs from Shannon on Monday."

"Monday," Henry reiterated.

"Yes, and she's American you see. Fits right in, doesn't it? Now, you've got to get down here tomorrow."

"I can fly to Dublin on Saturday and have the rest of the week for my article," Henry suggested. "Look, I've got four pieces to complete before classes begin."

"No. That won't do at all. You must come tomorrow. We'll show her London and then Dublin. We must all be great friends by Sunday night. That's important if she's to help us. Anyhow, you'll honestly like her."

"If I like her I shall hate like hell to use her."

Ian's reply was flippant. "Just remind yourself of the rewards, dear chap."

He heard Henry James sigh and knew he was thinking of the directorship of the Brockhurst collection. He was also thinking too bad that crime does pay, or something equally banal. The trouble with the lower classes is that some of them have such damnable, admirable morals. Not that they were above stealing but they worried about it so much before and after. Ian had a close call on occasion and promised himself to stick to the legitimate, but the right and wrong of it never troubled him.

His hand was still on the receiver. He released it now and smiled as he took a sip of the drink the waiter had put down. Ian Hardwicke was not a chronic clubman but it was comforting to know there was one place where there could be no intrusion.

One million pounds. He could begin to count on it again.

"Kimberleigh Brennan." Ian repeated her name softly. "You dear thing." He lifted his glass and began to adjust the plan to fit her.

Henry James stowed his bag in the overhead compartment, removed his expensive tweed jacket and tucked it neatly on top. As he settled into the aisle seat he no more than glanced at the two men in the row but as soon as he fastened his seat belt he became uncomfortably aware of his well dressed companions. If he had been alone he would have put his coat on again. Though the strangers appeared to be absorbed in their morning papers, they might notice the action and think it odd. A gentleman would probably not have removed his coat. If he had, it would have been flung casually somewhere. That too careful consideration for his clothes was one thing that marked him as belonging to the lower classes. Why could he not learn that, as he had learned so many other things? No one would know from his speech that he had grown up in a small fishing village or that his father was barely literate. His credentials were acceptable, a public-school education and Trinity with honors. No need to mention that it was all because of scholarships. On most occasions he congratulated himself on his accomplishments but this morning he was dissatisfied. The article was not going as smoothly as he had hoped. Bosch was his specialty and it should have been simple.

There was still no letter in yesterday's post offering him the position. Two months ago when he applied, Ian had assured him that he was certain to get the directorship. The prestige he coveted appeared to have eluded him for the moment but St. Margaret's expected so little and it was comfortable. There was ample time for writing and it was, after all, his critical essays which were building his reputation. Henry thought contentedly of his career as a teacher. So he was in a small school for girls at this point. A very old, very good one and perhaps he would yet get the collection.

His mood improved and he could have dozed had not the man in the middle seat left the airplane at Newcastle. After Henry stood to let the chap into the aisle, he reached into the compartment for his coat. The costly, rough, handwoven fabric reminded him of how much of his life depended upon Ian Hardwicke. It was Ian who made the coat possible. Ian who had made so many things possible since that afternoon twenty-odd years ago when a tall, slim fellow stepped out of a Mercedes-Benz coupe in front of the Trinity gate. It was Henry's first day in Dublin. The chap asked him how to find the library. They chatted a bit and discovered they were to be in the same class. He thought then, and still thought, that Ian Hardwicke was the most relaxed, most assured, best dressed man he had ever met. Before he pointed out the library, which he had only just discovered himself, he vowed he would see more of his classmate.

Ian had been amused by the awkward lad at first, then flattered into giving him the benefit of his tutelage. Henry had known he would acquire a vast knowledge of art but he would never have been articulate enough to communicate this knowledge without Ian. Now he was equally at ease in a drawing room or on a lecture platform. Ian had opened social doors he had never known existed. In fact, it was because of Hardwicke's connections that St.Margaret's had hired a boy from the West of Ireland to give their young ladies at least a casual acquaintance with Michelangelo and Caravaggio and the French Impressionists.

Henry could barely remember when their relationship started to change. Perhaps it was over the La Tour. He had affirmed it, though it was not his period and there was a nagging doubt in his mind. After that, Ian didn't seem to worry about Henry's scruples. Without ever consciously making a decision aye or nay, Henry had become involved to the point that he was going to Dublin to verify a stolen art object so old, so rare, that he became lightheaded and dizzy when he thought about it. He had hesitated. He was not an antiquities expert. But the piece had great provenance. He had re-searched the period thoroughly. He had been to Dublin to look at the piece now three times. He was certain he could authenticate it. A "mystery" buyer in the States was going to pay a million pounds to keep it in a vault and presumably look at it in the wee hours of particularly dark nights.

Perhaps it was all relative after all, Henry sighed. Was Ian really more guilty than the rich American who was hiding something so precious? To possess that which should belong to the world? To banish a part of man's history?

If only Kim whatever-her-name-was could get it into the United States. Ian Hardwicke was a criminal. (Or was he only a criminal after the police had apprehended him?) At any rate, he was a thief. On a monumental scale. But Henry would accept his share of the money, just as he had accepted the appointment at St. Margaret's and the possibility of the Brockhurst collection. He was as guilty as Ian. He had convinced himself in the beginning that he was not really involved. He was only identifying works of art as authentic, and any art historian might have done the same. But he knew this was nonsense. He was an accomplice to crime.

The cabin attendant announced luncheon and Henry was glad of the distraction. He sipped a Scotch and soda and then nibbled the gammon and carrots. He never minded airline food like most others did. Actually he was hungry but Ian had said they would have lunch. He managed to doze and think of nothing for the rest of the flight.

When the aircraft touched the runway he pulled down his bag and rested it on the seat beside him. He carefully straightened his collar and tie and his fingers moved quickly, smoothing his crisp reddish hair. Anyone glancing at him casually would say a slightly burly, tweedily well-dressed visitor was coming to town. Few would peg him as an art teacher.

Henry saw Ian towering above the others waiting at the gate. The tall woman with the smile must be Sydney. He couldn't see her legs. Ian had said they were a bit thin. As he moved through the crowd he spotted Kim, the much shorter figure standing between them.

"My God, she *is* beautiful," he murmured. He could tell he was going to be dull and silent.

Ian seemed a little too hearty, he thought. Sydney offered a firm handshake and Kim continued a monologue about a restaurant in Florence as they piled into Ian's Silver Cloud.

"Well, I've finally discovered a way to keep Kim from talking," Sydney said. "Just feed her chicken and almonds."

They were lunching in the charming inn Ian had chosen off the beaten path.

"Do they always give you such mounds of food?" Kim asked happily.

"Always," Ian answered. "There's a repertory theatre nearby so this is an actor's hangout and the portions are enormous. Apparently actors are a hungry lot. I brought you two here for sentimental reasons."

"Kim, this reminds me of that restaurant we found the time I visited you when you were doing *The Women*."

She explained to Ian and Henry, "You know that old warhorse with a big cast, all women. They were playing in some ghastly barn in Massachusetts. There were about twelve girls sharing a dressing room with only a couple of mirrors.

"Kim was an apprentice and all excited by the glamour of the theatre and she was driving everyone crazy with questions. Finally they made her pay a fine of a quarter every time she interrupted. She came up with enough questions to buy champagne for the whole cast Saturday night while they struck the set." She turned to Kim and smiled affectionately. "Actually everyone adored her. It was a lot of fun that week."

"You were outrageous. Remember?"

"It really was ridiculous," Sydney admitted. "After all, I was an established actress—years of credits behind me, even a reputation of sorts—but I suppose I was getting disenchanted with the theatre because I was cutting up like a school girl. The actress who was playing Crystal came down with laryngitis and I stepped in."

"The company manager called a meeting after the show one night and lectured us about having a better time than the audience. I was afraid I'd be fired," Kim recalled.

"Or reported to Equity, which was even worse," Sydney added. "How seriously we took Equity."

"The actors' union, you know," Kim explained.

"Yes, we've heard of it," Ian commented dryly.

"I was notorious in those days," Sydney admitted.

"For?"

"Practical jokes."

Kim groaned, remembering.

"You?" Ian asked with incredulity. "Practical jokes? I'm aghast, darling. You seem much too chic for that sort of thing."

"Now you know my weakness. There was a lot of telephoning in the play. I bribed an electrician who had a crush on me to hook up the phone for real and then got on the other end during someone's big scene."

Kim howled. "Remember how Sylvia broke up?"

"And how mad she was! We were idiots."

"Remember the time you were doing a commercial in Astoria and you invited me to come out?"

Sydney nodded.

"When I stepped off the train this belligerent policeman took my arm and said, 'This way,' and led me off. I was terrified. Of course the explanation was that Sydney arrived early and struck up a conversation with the cop and persuaded him to play a joke."

"Every time we were out of town," Sydney joined in, "we'd write a postcard with a blunt pencil to some ostentatious actress saying, *I seen your name in the washroom in the bus station in Chicago. I'm lonesome to.*"

If Ian and Henry failed to appreciate the reminiscent humor of their long ago pranks, they still smiled politely.

While they were laughing at themselves, Kim caught Ian eyeing her in an appraising way which made her feel uneasy.

"Enough of that," Sydney said at last. "Don't fret, I hardly indulge in jokes anymore. I have one friend, Walter Carrasco, who encourages me to think of outrageous tricks. He's a practical joker himself, or would be if his profession allowed it."

Kim was about to ask what his profession was when Ian took out his thin gold pocket watch. "I'm glad I don't bring that side of your nature to the fore. We must be getting back to town. I have an unforgettable evening planned for us. A concert is included, that's all I'm going to tell you."

Henry could anticipate Ian's annoyance when he learned that he had not brought evening clothes. Not even a dark suit, actually.

He sat quietly in the back seat beside Kim as the big car purred along and Ian told anecdotes about neighborhoods and streets and pubs they passed.

Kim smiled at him from time to time. He had an almost uncontrollable urge to reach over and take her hand. Or to kiss her. Be honest, he told himself. You want more to hold than that dainty hand.

 **4**

Of course the musicians were world class, the hall aglitter,the audience pretty and polished.

Afterward Ian was charming and knowledgeable as he spun yarns about composers and compositions as they savored their supper.

Sydney was witty. Kim was intrigued by it all. Henry was quiet, perhaps a little sullen, uncomfortable in his tweed jacket.

All in all though, it was the perfect evening Ian had promised. Anyone meeting them as they strolled companionably arm-in-arm through Soho might have remarked on the attractive foursome who were obviously close friends.

"Ah, let's stop in here." Ian slowed their progress. "This man called Calcularius is remarkable. He is without a doubt the best conjurer I have ever encountered."

"Conjurer?" Kim asked. "Magic?"

"Yes, of course my dear. But conjuring, you know, implies that it's for entertainment."

Suddenly Kim knew why she did not quite like Ian. Behind the ready smile, the smooth exterior, was almost always a sneer. A putdown.

"And for entertainment," Ian continued, "this fellow can hardly be surpassed. Come. You'll see."

It was a nightclub like any other but the stage was bare except for a lone, elongated figure who seemed not to belong to this world but to have stepped in a perfected state from a painting into the spotlight. His dark hair was combed straight back, his face blue or, more accurately, blue-white. His mouth was very red. He had wings, sheer, almost white, with eyes in them as if they helped him see. But he also had arms. The arms and, in fact, his whole body, were encased in grey, something between a union suit his grandfather might have worn and the sleek, body-moulded costumes adopted by Olympic athletes. He wore red boots which were winged, or seemed to be. As he moved toward the front of the stage the illusion was that he might soar.

"How old is Calcularius?" His voice was high pitched, almost falsetto. Ian whispered, "This is the only time he speaks during the entire performance."

"I am ancient. My ancestors practiced magical arts in the temples, in the theatres. My name—Calcularius—is an old Roman word meaning he who deals with pebbles. I am called after my ancestors."

Ian was explaining again. "He does the old cups and balls trick better than anyone I've ever seen. Of course he uses pebbles instead of balls—in memory of his ancestors." He chuckled. "As you know, it is one of the oldest tricks around. The Egyptians knew a version of it, the Chinese, all of Europe."

"I am young, I am naive, I am fresh, I am pliable. I am any age you wish me to be," Calcularius continued in his unusual high voice.

"Let me amuse you. Let me amaze you. Let me frighten you. Let me entertain you."

He seemed to walk on tiptoe as he glided through the audience. Smiling. Perhaps not smiling but seeming to smile. Rotund matrons almost swooned when he paused beside them. A girl giggled as he kissed her firm young hand.

Calcularius paused before a pleasant looking middle-aged couple. With a flourish he placed three inverted cups on the tiny round table beside them. Without speaking, using only gestures and flourishes and facile changes of expression, he held them spellbound as the pebble mysteriously jumped invisibly from cup to cup and then multiplied into three pebbles.

"The success of this trick usually relies heavily upon distracting conversation by the conjurer. What's so remarkable about this fellow is that he doesn't speak," Ian whispered. "Of course the basis for the trick is a secret additional pebble which by skilled manipulation is placed under one cup while the known pebble is removed from another."

Kim wished he wouldn't explain. The enchantment was lessened.

But Ian was caught up in the excitement of the performance. "Many people think conjuring depends upon the quickness of the hand deceiving the eye. Not so. The tricks are designed primarily to fool the mind. He is directing attention toward one action rather than away from another. Most anyone watching a good performer at work will take no notice of many things the eyes can actually see. Calcularius of course has great dexterity. I've watched him often. His precision and timing are phenomenal."

"I think you're a frustrated magician, luv. You missed your calling." Sydney laughed as she patted his wrist affectionately.

"Perhaps. I first saw this fellow years ago in a bar in Cork City. He was good then, but over the years he has honed his skills remarkably. You'll see when he returns to the stage."

Calcularius was now smiling at a pale thin grey woman as he removed a keepsake from her fragile wrist. Then he noticed Ian seated at the next table. For perhaps two seconds he lost his concentration. It was long enough for the woman to notice, though she did not know why she felt uneasy for an instant. In spite of the hesitation, the bauble slipped easily into his pocket. Still he hated the distraction. Not as much as he hated Ian Hardwicke.

Ian ordered champagne. Very dry, just old enough, expensive. The note he sent to Calcularius on a folded napkin said only, *Do join us*.

Calcularius returned to the spotlight at the front of the small stage. He smiled as he held up, one after another, a diamond necklace, a family heirloom, a wallet, the bauble he had almost faltered in removing. He did not need to speak. The exclamations from the owners and the audience applause spoke for him.

Kim clapped her hands with almost childlike glee. "Will he do tricks when he joins us?"

"Perhaps. He plays with coins, cards. He's a juggler, reads palms. One of the keys to his success is that you can never anticipate which tricks he'll use. However, he always returns to the stage with his pockets full of items he has lifted." Ian glanced around. Calcularius was gliding through a door at stage left. "Excuse me for a moment."

He returned with the magician in tow. Ian drew up a chair from an empty table and motioned for the waiter to pour champagne for the performer.

"Why do you paint your face blue—or white?" Kim asked as she studied him, now that he was closer.

He smiled shyly. "I can see them and they can't see me." His voice had the same pitch so noticeable on stage.

"Be a good fellow, read our palms." Ian reached for Sydney's hand. She jerked her fingers out of his grasp.

"No. Absolutely not."

"Come on," Ian coaxed. "You're not superstitious. Don't tell me. You can't be serious."

"My friends often tell me they can't tell when I'm serious. My detractors say it's because I'm so shallow." She was trying to be light but not pulling it off well. "Anyhow, I'm serious about this. I will not have my palm read. I've had my fortune told twice. Never again. I don't want to talk about it. Don't want to think about it."

She excused herself.

After a moment, Kim followed. Sydney was pacing in front of the long gilt mirror in the powder room.

"You all right?" Instantly Kim wondered why one always asked that question of someone who obviously is not all right.

"I will be in a moment, luv. Run on back to the table. I'll be along."

5 It was almost three a.m. when they returned to Sydney's hotel and the lift was not running.

"Are you inviting us up for a drink?"

"Oh, Jesus, no. I have to be up at daylight to check on some material."

"Daylight?"

"Well, I'll be out of here by ten or a little after."

Ian kissed both Sydney and Kim goodnight.

Henry shook hands, holding Kim's a moment longer than necessary as he said, "I'll stop for you tomorrow morning for the Changing of the Guard—around ten."

"Great. I'll be ready."

As they wearily climbed the five flights, Kim sighed. "You know Henry is almost exactly the same size as Scott."

"So?"

"I don't know, it makes him seem so safe and dependable somehow."

"In the same way Scott was dependable?"

Kim winced. "Ooh, I asked for that."

"Sorry. I'm afraid it seems to me he turned out to be a real jerk."

"I shouldn't have mentioned him. I think I'm getting over it all and then I meet a nice man like Henry and I get uneasy. I like Henry, I feel at ease with him. Are you sure he's not someone's husband?"

"Kim, for heavens sake, there are all sorts of men around who aren't husbands. How did *you* ever get so wifely? You sound as if you've been married for decades."

"I know, I know. It frightens me. I can't remember what it was like before I was with Scott and we weren't even married. It's fun to be here. I feel free and irresponsible."

"Is that good?"

"I think so. It's not that I wasn't happy with Scott but everyone pegged me as his. We were very happy really...only...."

"Only you didn't eat truffles and drink a fine Montrachet every night, right?"

"Once in a while we had a big night out but that wasn't Scott's idea of fun. He liked pizza and a ball game. Do you really live like this all the time?"

"As a matter of fact, I do. Just like tonight. Concerts, dinner, all-night clubs—the whole bit. And you know what?"

"What?"

"I'm not in the least tired of it."

Kim laughed.

Sydney turned to her as she twisted the key in the lock. "You know, after Townie died, I felt pretty sorry for myself. I went into a complete slump. And my friends were so awed by widowhood that they left me alone. I began to think about the rest of my life. I was barely forty. I didn't want to go back into the theatre as an actress after being the producer's wife. You know what that would be like. And, let's face it, I wasn't a really big name anyhow. I saw myself stepping into all those brave and brittle middle-aged parts and I said to myself—Sydney old girl this is where you get out. You're not a star and you never will be. You're just a gaudy half-talent that sparkles quite a lot and you need to get some fun out of life before that sparkle dims. So I began to think of what I could do to be able to afford this life. We lived splendidly while Townie was alive and he left me plenty if I were careful, but who wants to be careful."

"All you ever wanted was a simple mink coat, a simple diamond watch, a simple sports car as I remember."

"Uh huh, that's the truth—all the luxuries and none of the necessities, as the old saying goes. I rather fell into decorating. You know how people tell you that you write such wonderful letters you should be a writer. Well, they always asked me who was my decorator. It started me thinking. I had a completely untrained gift for rooms and houses. I could put chairs and lamps and curtains together and come up with something. So, I hid away in the custom decorating department of a big store for about a year and learned the fundamentals from all the sweet clever boys there."

They sat side by side on the deep sofa facing the balcony and sipped the nightcaps Sydney had poured.

"Oh, I need this," Kim said. "If I keep drinking like this I will be so hung over I'll miss the rest of my stay in London."

"Just so you sober up in time for Dublin. You can start fresh again in true Irish style."

"Sydney," Kim paused for a moment. "You were so upset over the palm reading. I was worried about you. Is it all right to ask?"

"I suppose so. I don't talk about it often. Or easily." She grinned. "I told your father and he was on the one hand, very understanding and, on the other, has teased me since, but very gently."

Kim waited.

"You didn't know my mother. She was wonderfully creative and loads of fun but her judgment was sometimes questionable. Anyhow, for my eleventh birthday she decided to take me and three or four friends to a fortune teller. What an intriguing idea. We were all atwitter. We arrived at her door giggling and wondering which boys in the class she'd pair us with and whether she'd know we hated our math teacher. We were not nearly sophisticated enough to wonder about tall dark strangers or mysterious happenings. Mother made it clear to me that even though it was my birthday I was the hostess and should be last.

"Madame Eulalie, I still remember her name, was good. She told my girl friends about boys who liked them and wouldn't admit it, good grades and incidents at camp. It was entertaining and completely innocuous.

"She held my hand and turned it to different angles. She frowned.

"'My dear,' she said at last, 'do be careful about husbands. You'll survive them all.'

"Of course my companions squealed with delight. One of the quick ones caught the plural of husbands and shrieked from excitement.

"I've been to a fortune teller only one other time—when I was in college. Don't ask me why I went again. This one was more sinister than Madame Eulalie. She was seated at a small table in the corner of a dark bar with a sign that advertised fortunes for five dollars. I was having a beer with an intense boy from my Shakespeare class and he thought we should consult her.

"He insisted I go first, but I urged him and finally she signaled for him to be first.

"She asked him a couple of questions and then told him he would be a famous actor. Even I could have listened to his too cultivated voice and figured that was his dream.

"When it was my turn she shuffled the cards with a few flourishes and then laid them out.

"She studied the black ladies in the first row and some other cards which no doubt had significance and finally told me to be careful. To think before I married. She said I'd have three husbands and all would die before me, under unusual circumstances."

Sydney took a deep breath. "Then she looked up at me. She seemed somehow puzzled as if she'd been surprised—disturbed—by what she had seen in the cards. I'm sure I seemed much too young for such a prediction.

"She then shuffled the cards hastily and dismissed us.

"As you can imagine, I remembered her prediction when Pearson was killed in Vietnam. That was a long time ago. You probably don't remember about it."

"Vaguely."

"We were living in a funny little basement place in The Village. Happy as could be. I was getting some small parts and he was working for *The Voice*. He even had a by-line now and then and expected to be a big-name journalist. Probably would have been. He was a good writer. It was a war he didn't believe in but of course he jumped at a chance to cover it.

"He arrived in Hue in mid-January, almost on the eve of the battle. There was an uneasy truce so everyone was jittery, but it was also a time of religious and family celebrations as the new year approached—incidentally, the Year of the Monkey which the wise ones said would bring bad luck.

"Pearson was taken with the city. I received one letter in which he described the old city and the emperor's palace and the interesting mixture of Vietnamese and French influence.

"He filed one story about Hue on the eve of the battle. It told about the fear and tension and danger but also about the neat gardens in the suburbs.

"A few days later he paused to look over a garden wall for a moment and his head was blown off." There was a long silence. "At least that's what they told me. Anyhow the circumstances were unusual as the fortune teller predicted.

"Then years went by. It is wonderful how time blurs things. But you know those words haunted me again in nightmares after Townie collapsed on an opening night and died two days later, just before his sixtieth birthday. You can bet I'll never marry again." Sydney swallowed the last of her drink and left the room.

Kim wondered why she had been so completely silent, not even an "hm," or an "ah," or an "oh" during the telling. But what could she have said, or asked. It was all too weird.

6   They were finishing a late breakfast when Henry stopped by.

"Join us?" he invited

"No thanks, luvs. I've seen it many times, always with a lump in my throat too. I've got to check measurements on curtains before I go to Dublin. If they're off a sixteenth of an inch it'll be curtains for me. And I must call and get tickets for the Abbey. Kim would never forgive me if she didn't see a performance."

"You're a bit late already," Henry commented. "It's not the theatre it once was."

"In *your* day?" teased Sydney. "Next you'll tell us you knew Lady Gregory."

"Not really," he grinned boyishly, "but I went often when I was at Trinity. I saw everything—*Juno, Playboy, Shadow of a Gunman.* Marvelous."

"Dear hearts, I hate to break in on these misty-eyed sentiments, but the Guards don't wait for anyone. If you want to get up front before all the American tourists crowd you out, you'd better dash."

Kim collected herself in haste and they were off. As the door closed she was telling Henry all she had read and heard about the Changing of the Guard. Sydney laughed to herself as she searched for the ringing telephone and caught it at the third buzz.

"Sydney, old dear, can you meet me for a little drink around four o'clock?"

"Ian, I'd love to, but I have to check some measurements this afternoon. I've been lazy all morning. I should have been ready to go out when Kim and Henry left."

"It's frightfully important. I know we'll all be together tonight but I need to see you—alone. Just for a few minutes."

His voice was insistent and at the same time apologetic so she agreed.

As they hurried through Green Park Kim exclaimed over the acres of green grass.

"And this has been an extremely dry year," Henry said. "You should see it after rains. This is the smallest of the Royal Parks. It's the only one without a lake or flowers. It was created in the 1660s on what had been a burial ground for lepers."

They were not ahead of the tourists but Henry found a spot on the Victoria Monument which he assured her was the very best view. The Scottish regimental band, kilted and playing bagpipes, delighted Kim. The event was all she had imagined.

At the end of the ceremony Henry took her hand and guided her through the crowd.

"Just near here is a pub you'll like, I think. It's frequented by—depending upon the time of day or night—Palace guards, staff, servants. No pretensions, good hearty fare."

"I didn't think I'd be the least bit hungry after a late breakfast but I am. All this walking."

The fare was indeed hearty she observed as they sipped pints and settled in to enjoy roast beef sandwiches.

Kim thought a moment as she ate. She looked carefully at Henry. Started to speak. Hesitated. Decided she liked him quite a lot. Decided he was trustworthy.

"Something has been bothering me ever since last night."

"What?"

"That man—the magician—Calcularius. I don't think he likes Ian. Or, he's afraid of him. Something strange."

Henry pondered before he answered. Which was like him. "Really. I didn't notice anything to suggest that. Ian barely knows him I think. Only as a performer. What seemed unusual?"

"I don't know. People always think I'm not paying attention and that I talk rather than listen but now and then I pick up something by, I don't know, intuition I guess."

"I couldn't even see any expression on his face with all that makeup. I'm sure I wouldn't recognize him if he walked through that door."

"Oh, I couldn't either. He wouldn't want us to recognize him. Remember when I asked why he painted his face he told me so he could see them and they couldn't see him. No, it wasn't any expression on his face. Call it body language, I suppose. He didn't seem to want to be at our table. Now that I look back on it, he didn't seem to want to be near Ian."

"Perhaps I'm just insensitive." He patted her hand. "Or perhaps your imagination is too vivid. However, it was obvious that Sydney didn't want Calcularius at our table. What was all that aversion to having her palm read. She must be frightfully superstitious."

Kim waited. "I don't know really," she finally answered.

"Well, enough speculation. I want to show you a park or two. London parks are first rate for people and dog watching and walking. When we're tired we can sit by the Serpentine."

And that's what they did for the better part of two hours.

"Queen Caroline had the Serpentine formed in the early 1700s from the flow of the Westbourne River. Almost a century later, in 1816, Shelley's wife drowned herself here."

Kim laughed. "You know so much about the parks. A while ago it was grass over a cemetery for lepers. You manage to make it all interesting. Like a tour guide. A very good one."

"I have a confession. When I came to London just after college I *was* a tour guide."

From that they backed up to his childhood.

"I hated the thought of being a fisherman. But that's what the men in my family had done for as long as could be remembered. My father took me in the boat before I was six." He grinned at her and shook his head. "The sea terrified me. Still does.

"I was good at boxing and I did well in school. My father thought that being able to fight might be useful, but he was convinced school was a waste.

"Some years were better than others but none were prosperous. I was working by the time I was nine or so but my mother managed to keep me in school.

"My father, who feared neither wind nor waves nor cold, came back from the sea one night in January, coughing. He went out the next day as always but the following day he stayed in bed. He never got up again. By February he was in hospital. With the coming of spring, instead of getting better, he died.

"I was twelve." He was obviously not accustomed to talking about himself or his childhood. "Enough of that," he said abruptly.

"Oh no. What happened next?" Kim's interest was genuine.

"Thanks to my mother and Father Patrick, the village priest, I stayed in school. I began to win prizes and get scholarships. Eventually it led to Trinity and then my coming to London to launch my career guiding tourists."

Suddenly he snapped his fingers. "I have an idea." He leaned over and placed both hands on the arms of her chair. "Let me show you London. Tonight. Properly."

"We're supposed to be having dinner with Sydney and Ian."

"We'll ring them. They can have a good evening without us, I'm certain."

He looked at his watch. "First place I'm taking you is Harrods. Before they close. You can ring Sydney from there."

They walked quickly out of the park and along Brompton Road.He held her arm protectively as he guided her through traffic.

"You won't believe the size of the place. There are around 50,000 shoppers every day."

Kim couldn't believe it and declared she wished they could have spent the day there. "But then we'd have missed the Changing of the Guard and I wouldn't trade that for anything." She found a bright blue shirt she had to have for her mother and Henry had to drag her away from the toys.

"We didn't get to see anywhere near all of it. There's meat and vegetables and flowers There's a travel agency and a bank. Even a pub.

"Some of the other stores are more chic and glamorous I suppose. Like Selfridges and Liberty and, by all means, Harvey Nichols. But my favorite is Harrods. Can you guess what their motto is?"

"Not possibly."

"*Omnia Omnibus Ubique*—loosely, all things, for all people. Ah, there's a telephone."

7

The chore took longer than Sydney anticipated. Didn't they always? This was the tedious underpinning of an otherwise exciting profession. She was glad she had an excuse to duck out just before four o'clock.

She arrived at the little bar in Duke Street ahead of Ian, ordered a gin and tonic and settled back in a comfortable rattan chair. Why was he so edgy and restless lately—unlike him. The other day there was something important he had to say, she recalled, but he never got around to it. Could it be the Carleton Place decorating job had fallen through? Was he trying to find a kind way to tell her? Unconsciously she glanced down at her right hand. The ring had a green stone the size of a small marble. As she admired it she thought of the letter she had received this very week asking for payment.

"Oh good, you've ordered a drink already." Ian and the waiter arrived at the same instant. He approved of Sydney's choice. "This is a day for a gin and tonic; I'll have one as well."

Sydney Reardon had a healthy amount of curiosity but she had made up her mind before Ian arrived that she would not question him. If he wanted to be mysterious she would play along. He could reveal the reason for this clandestine meeting in his own good time. Her long fingers caressed the frosty glass and she waited.

"Cheers." Ian lifted the glass the waiter had just placed before him.

"Cheers."

"You're curious, no doubt, darling, about our secret meeting."

"Mildly," she replied lazily and smiled at him.

She's so frustratingly cool. Just how did he put this to her?

"I want you to do something for me and it's damned embarrassing to ask. Or actually, to have Kim do something for me."

Sydney waited. She was not going to help by asking questions.

"I have a client in the States. Connecticut. Rich, but God, so difficult. One of those captains of industry you read about." He looked into Sydney's eyes with great sincerity. "I have been trying to get a particular art object for his wife's birthday. Nothing really valuable, only a reproduction, but she has her heart set on it. The snare is that I must deliver it by Tuesday, for the celebration. When Kim said she was leaving on Monday it occurred to me she just might carry it. No bother for her, really. I will have someone come to her hotel in New York to collect it."

"I'm sure she'd be glad to take it. Why ask me? Why not just ask her directly?"

"There are other minor difficulties. The damn thing is not really old enough to be authenticated as an antique." He gestured in an offhand way. "Misses by perhaps a decade. This man, this rich man, balks at details. I do not mind having it packed for shipping, paying the duty and all but because of the time element I need to get it there right away."

Sydney pondered. "I'd do it in a minute but I'm not sure about Kim. I think it may sound like smuggling to her. You can't imagine how honest she is."

"Hm. I gathered that just getting to know her. Do you feel it's really dishonest?"

"Of course not. I told you it wouldn't bother me. In fact, I must be dishonest by nature. I love the thrill of minor smuggling. I always bring firecrackers back from Mexico just for fun. And once I smuggled a parrot into the U.S. from Panama." She shook her head, smiling ruefully. "But I just don't know about Kim."

"I wouldn't ask but it's important. He's so frightfully...." He searched for the proper word. "Quixotic. It seems essential that he have this for his wife's birthday. I'm hoping to sell him something really valuable one day if I can keep him interested. He likes art—has a couple of minor Impressionists. He's working up to being a very good client. *You* know how this sort of thing is." He was appealing to her professional instincts.

"Oh, Jesus, don't I!" She sighed. "Perfectly. Let me think it over." Sydney rose. "I must dash. The man was to have left word about our Abbey tickets but if he hasn't, I'll need to make another call. Why do I always leave arrangements to the last moment? Of course I anticipated the

Shelbourne would have a variety of rooms. But no. Kim and I are in one together. I haven't shared a room with a girl since my summer theatre days."

"I could probably get you in at my place."

"Thanks. We'll be fine. It's not for long."

He walked with her to the curb and hailed a taxi.

"About the birthday gift," he said as he closed the door. "You will work something out?"

"I'll try."

"We'll stop for you around eight. I think Kim will like the evening I've planned."

Poor old Ian, Sydney mused as her taxi wound its way through late afternoon shopping traffic along Oxford Street. There are so many troublesome headaches in business. Like the silly birthday gift. It's those annoying details that plagued her as a decorator too. Why can't you depend on anyone? Last week she was sure the weaver in Dublin knew the pattern perfectly and now she was making another trip. Thank God Carleton Place was not the problem. She'd try to get Kim to help him.

Even when she didn't really want to bother, Sydney always checked for messages. Probably a holdover from acting days when a call could mean a part.

Henry is showing me London. Properly. Tonight, the message from Kim said. *Sorry to miss dinner with you and Ian. Please forgive. See you later.*

"When was this message left?" Sydney asked the hotel operator. "There's no time indicated."

"Within the hour. I'm so sorry, Miss Reardon. That new girl."

Is Kim interested in Henry? He is nice enough but so quiet.

"Hello luv," Sydney said when Ian answered. "You and I are going to be alone tonight. Not that I don't always welcome an evening with you."

"I'll enjoy that. But why?"

"Henry is showing Kim London. Properly. Tonight, the message says."

Ian chuckled. Old Henry was warming to his assignment. "I'll call for you around eight."

 **8** Walter Carrasco had followed instructions implicitly. But there was no one there. What had started out to be a routine transaction had turned into a waiting game. He hated that. After almost two hours he had gone to the hotel and telephoned.

"Don't leave the room until you hear from me," The Boss said. One thing Walter had known for a long time, you never go against orders.

There were only so many things you could do in a hotel room. He sighed and turned back to the storybook girl on the bed.

She was young with golden red hair, rich and smelled of expensive perfume. And, unlikely as it seemed, she was mad for a guy she had met not long ago in a hotel bar.

She didn't wait for him. She was opening his shirt, unzipping his fly and snapping the waist button so she could tug at his trousers. At the same time she was unfastening her skirt. When he pulled it off he saw she was naked from the waist down. A groan escaped his lips as he caressed her breasts with one hand while the other moved down to her honey-red cunt. Her mouth found his and her tongue moved playfully around. Now she was over him, under him, tantalizing, demanding. It was a new experience for him and he thought he was experienced.

The love scene was unreal. Nothing but crap.

Walter flung the book across the room. But he had a hard-on that made him moan. That was for real.

The telephone rang. Where the hell had he put it?

"I want you in Dublin by ten tomorrow morning. You'll get instructions at the hotel."

That was all there was to the conversation. When The Boss was that curt, things were not going well.

Walter showered and went downstairs for a bite to eat. Then he'd check on early flights to Ireland.

He settled on a stool at the long bar. There was a girl three seats away. She was quite pretty, not too young and he could bet she was not rich. She smiled at him.

He'd never picked up one of those books with cheap paper and bad writing in an airport before. It was completely unbelievable and yet he was still remembering the scene.

"You look lonely, my friend. Would you like to buy me a drink?"

She did not yet know that a drink was all he was buying tonight. If there was one thing The Boss made clear it was that business and pleasure don't mix. And he was definitely on a business trip.

He smiled at her. "Why not? Just one. I still have work to do." He wanted to be sure he made their very brief relationship clear.

It was just dusk as Henry and Kim strolled toward the spot where he'd told her he wanted to live.

"Here it is, Belgrave Square."

"Charming. They remind me of row houses in Baltimore."

"I want to spend my old age looking out on that unlikely statue of Bolivar." They walked over and sat on the base.

"You're right that London is great for people watching. Look at that couple. She can't be more than, what, early twenties, and he's got to be in his sixties."

"He's her grandfather."

Kim laughed. "I'll bet. If he is, he's excessively affectionate"

"She's his nurse. His keeper."

"Then she's pretty unprofessional. She just kissed him."

"So? You don't want him to have any fun because he needs a keeper?"

"Alas. We'll never know."

They were distracted by three boys in school uniforms having a fierce tug of war over a soccer ball.

"I'm glad you like people watching. It's one of my favorite sports. Let's go to Trafalgar Square. You'll find it most pleasant at this hour with the lights and the fountains.

"This is the true center of London, emotionally as well as geographically," Henry was saying as they stepped down from the taxi. "Would you like me to stop? The way I'm rambling on I must have missed being a tour guide."

"Don't stop, I love it."

He pointed out St. Martin-in-the-Fields and the National Gallery.

"Originally over there at the end of the square where there's a statue of Charles I, there was a cross erected in 1291 by Edward I. It marked the final resting place of the funeral procession of his queen, Caroline. 'Charing' is a corruption of the French *chere reine*, 'dear queen.' Anyhow, there's a later cross from the 19th century in front of the station. All distances in London are measured from the site of the original one."

They were sauntering toward the Nelson column. "The story goes that when they cleaned the column and the statue not too long ago, they removed a ton of pigeon droppings. That's the trivia for today.

"I want to take you to The Dove for dinner. It's an old pub beside the river. Wonderful on the terrace this time of year. But it's a long ride—let me ring to be certain of a table."

They had dined and taxied and walked along the Embankment. Somehow she lost track of the hours. Still leaning against Henry's shoulder she opened her eyes and drowsily watched launches rubbing lethargically against the dock. Big Ben struck three o'clock.

"You had a nice nap," Henry said and kissed the top of her head lightly. "Are you warm enough? Would you like my coat?"

"No, I'm fine, thanks." She turned so she could look at him.

His arms tightened around her and he was kissing her, gently at first and then hungrily. She returned the embrace.

In a moment they were lying on the damp grass locked in one another's arms, their mouths seeking, their hands exploring.

There was a tap-tap on the walk and the sound of heavy boots.

"Move along now," a deep, not unkind, voice was saying and a Bobby was silhouetted against the sky.

They scrambled up hand-in-hand and disappeared behind a clump of bushes. As they turned, the policeman was strolling away and a weary drunk who had heaved himself up from a bench was waiting a few moments before settling in again.

Realizing suddenly that they were not the culprits, they began to giggle like naughty school children. They clasped hands and swung round and round together until they fell to the ground too dizzy to stand.

Henry kissed her companionably. "That was nice. Could have been nicer without that Bobby."

Kim wasn't the least shy as she said, "It will be nice in the right time and place."

"You've had a snooze, you're all rested so let's walk for a while until we find a taxi. There aren't too many about at this hour."

They walked a long way. Hardly talking. Getting to feel comfortable with one another.

"New Covent Garden Market," Henry said when they finally hailed a taxi. Still the tour guide, during the ride he explained that the new market was not so colorful as the old. "But I expect it is more efficient."

The Barley Mow was just welcoming its first customers of the new morning. Greengrocers there for vegetables and fruits and flowers.

"Some of these chaps have been working since three or four o'clock and they're ready to eat. We are too, I should think."

"I'm starving."

"Good. And remember, Courage is the drink of the house."

"At this hour?"

"Of course. It will go down well with a full breakfast."

At around seven-thirty Friday morning Kim knocked and Sydney sleepily made her way to open the door.

"I can explain," Kim began. "I had the most wonderful time. We were up all night and...."

"No, no, no, dear heart. Don't give me the details. If you tell all you'll be sorry tomorrow. I'm assuming something happened. At least I hope so."

"No, it didn't. It might have except for the policeman." Kim paused. "Actually, I think something *did* happen. Something important. I learned about Henry. And, I told him about Scott and me and he understood."

Sydney would not have been telling the truth if she'd said she was not curious. Though she'd never admit it.

"You'd better get a little sleep. Our flight doesn't leave until two-something. I don't want you to fall asleep before the end of the first act tonight."

"You don't have to persuade me. Be sure to wake me in time to get dressed and pack," Kim called over her shoulder as she moved toward her room.

10 The Aer Lingus jet was crowded on this pre-weekend afternoon. They were passing through heavy clouds most of the way, but as they were beginning the descent for landing, the sun suddenly broke through. Kim looked down at the incredibly verdant fields separated by hedgerows, neat and glistening and somehow familiar, and she burst into noisy sobs. The cabin attendant was accustomed to sentimental Americans of Irish extraction and she smiled in sympathy. Sydney leaned over and kissed Kim's cheek.

"Always makes me want to cry. Did you ever read that book, *It's a Funny Country in a Sad Kind of Way*? Or maybe it's the other way around, a sad country in a funny kind of way. Anyhow, it's all about a writer who brings his children to live in Ireland for a time and the little boy describes the country that way."

"I'll read it." Kim was wiping her eyes and pulling herself together as they touched the runway.

By the time they collected bags and umbrellas and found a taxi, the weather had again undergone one of those startling changes that are commonplace in the Emerald Isle. A harsh wind had sprung up sweeping sheets of cold rain along the streets. The wipers on the windscreen groaned asthmatically and Sydney was busy drying her new black patent attaché case with an inadequate lace hanky.

The driver was a sour-faced dyspeptic whose bravado driving of his wheezing vehicle made even Sydney look up anxiously. He rounded corners with careless aplomb, slammed on brakes, ignored pedestrians. The afternoon bicycle traffic was at its height. Riders dipped and swerved and Kim peered through the steamed-over window in terror but the driver paid them no mind even when they shot across his path. He kept up a stream of acerbic comments on the weather, tourists, the quality of horses at Leopardstown, riots and the state of the country. He did not seem to expect or welcome any response. After a grueling eternity he pulled up in front of the Shelbourne with a screeching of tires.

They sagged back on the seat with relief, looking for their belongings. Someone was making a clear place on a side window with a white-gloved hand and presently a smiling red face appeared. Simultaneously the door opened and a gigantic black umbrella flew up.

The doorman was saying, "There, there, having a spot of weather now, aren't we? Never you mind. Just get yourselves into the lounge for a cup of tea and it will put you to rights in an instant. Oh, it's Missus Reardon is it. Too bad you weren't here last week for the fine weather. Go along now, I'll take care of the lot." And he swept up the bags and umbrellas and still managed to help them to the door.

"Missus Rear—don, please! Missus Rear—don."

The singsong voice floated in through the doorway as they lingered over tea in the lounge. The singer, clad in a shamrock green uniform, looked no more than eleven or twelve. His pants hit well above the ankles with the telltale white let-down line clearly visible. His bony wrists showed below green sleeves.

"Over here," Sydney called and gave him a tip and a bright smile.

"Thank you ma'am. A call for you."

"It must be my weavers. Oh, dear, what's happened *now*? Something ghastly, no doubt. Why did I ever get into the decorating business?" She jumped up, her short black hair bobbing as she followed the boy to the telephone.

Kim sipped the strong tea, happy to sit quietly for a time and ponder on being in Dublin. By the time Sydney returned she had decided she was going to adore Ireland.

"Not a problem. Just checking the time for our appointment tomorrow. Let's go up and get settled."

Kim had read about the Shelbourne but she was not prepared for the old-fashioned splendor. The room was huge by American standards, with a corner by the window furnished as a sitting room. The bathroom was almost as big as some motel rooms at home, with heated pipes for drying towels and a wonderful deep tub. The bath had an adjoining dressing room with a door opening to the outside hall. It disturbed her to find that. Although there were three locks, none seemed to hold very securely. "I'm glad I'm not in a room alone." She made Sydney go into the hall and try the door.

"Typical. We'll ask the room waiter to check the locks when he brings our tea."

"Tea? We just had tea! Enough to keep me awake for days."

"That was the drinking kind. To warm us after the downpour. Now we'll have the kind you eat. All sorts of sandwiches—on marvelous soda bread. Cakes, goodies, you know, the whole bit. The theatre starts early so there won't be time for dinner."

The waiter was an ancient bent man who recognized Sydney from other visits and was inclined to be loquacious. He looked over the locks casually and then agreed they didn't work well.

"So you've been in London, have you? Not a wonder you're worried about door locks." He gave Kim's shoulder a reassuring pat. "But you've no need to worry, luv. You're in Ireland now."

They laughed as they sat down to tea, served on carefully ironed linen and Georgian plate.

"You see what I mean about the Irish? Can you help loving them? Those locks have been broken since Thackeray stayed here. On the other hand, crimes of passion are rare. Everybody is too busy talking and drinking to do real violence. You don't hear much about murder unless it's drug related or political."

While Sydney made a couple of calls, Kim picked up a copy of the Irish Independent and read the personals with sympathy and amusement. "Listen to this. In the social notes. A relative of Saint Bernadette is visiting

Dublin this week. Did you ever think of a saint as having relations?"

"Aren't the papers incredible? And such editorial writing. Don't read the obits or you'll dissolve in tears."

They took their time dressing. The first performance for Kim at the Abbey was a big occasion.

Sydney opened a suede jewelry roll and pondered before making a decision.

"Wow! What a gorgeous ring!"

"Should be, dear heart. I bought it to hock as soon as I finish paying for it."

She put on earrings of intricately entwined gold and stones and several Florentined bracelets. Then she rolled up the case and tossed it in a drawer.

"Let's be off."

"You're not going to leave all that jewelry just lying in a drawer, are you? It's real, isn't it?"

"Of course it's real."

"But aren't you afraid somebody might steal it?"

"Wouldn't that be wonderful! It's not paid for, but it *is* insured. Then I'd get the money and I'd buy all new. I saw a divine bracelet...."

"Oh Sydney, don't you worry about anything? Except measurements?"

"But measurements are important. They're my work."

"You don't make sense. You spend hours making sure a curtain is exactly right, and then you throw thousands of dollars worth of jewelry aside and forget about it."

"Material things aren't all that important, are they? Anything money can buy isn't vital. *People* are important, my work is important. The things that make you care never have much to do with money, d'you think? Kindness—being good to people you love—laughing a lot—crying a little— living for each moment."

Was she thinking about Pearson, or Townie, Kim wondered. Was she still shaken over the fortune teller?

11

Danny O'Rahilly paused to look at the blowup.

CALCULARIUS
Conjurer
Magical Entertainment
Let him amaze you
Let him amuse you

It pleased him to stop in front of the club and look at the big poster. To think of his past. And, more important, of his future. Day after tomorrow he'd be in London. And the day after that he'd have his papers and be on the way to New York.

As he turned his back on the picture of himself, a waiter from the club brushed past him. It was always a surprise that even people who worked beside him did not recognize him once he removed the makeup. If he spoke they'd recognize him quickly enough. That falsetto had plagued him since that bus accident way back when he was twelve or thirteen.

No matter, it had served a good purpose. Otherwise he would never have worked out a routine with few words. And that was what set him apart from other performers. What he could do without repartee was remarkable, the critics agreed.

It may have served his professional life well but the voice made his personal life miserable.

"You sound like a fucking soprano," his father had remarked derisively. But every remark from his father was derisive.

The doctor said his high voice was the result of trauma. He needed professional help.

"Christ," his father said. "He wants to be a magician. Let him work magic on himself."

He looked at his watch and quickened his step as he moved toward the museum. Inside the hollow foyer he checked his watch against the big ornate clock above the stairs. Exactly sixteen minutes before the doors closed. He was wearing a dark jacket and cap. So were two-thirds of the other visitors. He took the thirty-one steps to the first landing at an even pace and turned right into the dim room where a small figure stood alone on a pedestal bathed in a circle of soft light. The voice announcing that the museum would close in fifteen minutes filled every corner of the building. He was looking at the most important piece in the collection. Everyone headed there on first entering. The room was empty now, as he had known it would be. As it had been at this hour on each of his earlier visits.

He looked at his watch again. The minutes would pass slowly. Vaulting over the ornate wooden railing was nothing; he could almost step over. Exchanging the figures was a matter of seconds with his deft fingers. His only worry was the electronic security device. It would be inoperative for exactly one minute, much more time than was required. If it was inoperative. Hardwicke had assured him that it would be. That was his responsibility and Danny was not to worry. But he did worry.

He strolled around the object, studying it from all angles. Ugly little creature, he thought, just as he had the first time he'd seen it. Must be worth plenty though, or Ian Hardwicke wouldn't be paying him ten thousand pounds and getting him papers.

He glanced around.

Only he and the little man on the pedestal were in the room.

He put one gloved hand on the railing and swung over. His soft-soled shoes made no sound on the marble floor. His heart pounded as he reached for the figure. There was no alarm. Hardwicke had done his part.

The metal figure was cold in his hand. The plaster replica he took from his pocket was warm.

How could he possibly have dropped it? The sound of the plaster breaking against the floor was deafening to him.

He was back over the railing, running toward the door before he drew up and moved slowly onto the top step. He looked behind and ahead, proceeding casually. In the foyer below, dozens of people were moving toward the exits. The hand on the bronze figure in his pocket was sweating.

Footsteps?

He could see the top of a uniform cap as a guard moved upward. He was old and climbed laboriously. He was big. Danny pulled the stocking concealed under his cap over his face. He hadn't intended to use it but now it seemed a precaution. No reason for the old man to recognize him. The attendant did not see him until they were almost side by side. He gasped. Danny pushed him aside and fled down the stairs, pulling the stocking away from his face. As the heavy body stumbled against the wall there was an oath.

At the last step Danny O'Rahilly slowed his pace to match the other visitors who were leaving. He did not start to run until he was around the corner and almost to the top of the street. And he did not stop running until he was in the little park by the river where he often read on warm days. He dropped to a bench, gasping for breath. He leaned forward and started to cradle his face in his hands. They were sweating so they slipped and he almost fell forward on the wet grass. He couldn't control the trembling and suddenly tears were streaming down his cheeks.

How long did he sit there in the drizzle crying?

Hours?

Twenty minutes by his watch.

He hadn't thought about how strange it must look to anyone passing by to see a man sitting on a park bench crying like a baby. But the clerks and housewives and school children hurrying along in the early evening mist gave him no thought.

With an effort he began to calm himself.

He had to get rid of the object. The instructions had been to leave it in a locker at the bus station. He had thought there'd be no particular hurry, but now there was. Had they already found the broken piece? He had planned to go directly to the club but now he couldn't.

He bought a newspaper and put it in the locker with the figure. He'd wrap it later before he delivered it. The station was still busy at this hour and no one paid any attention as he placed the locker key in his inside coat pocket and walked out.

The three-night stand in Dublin had seemed perfect when they offered it—a reason for being in town. He hadn't expected to need an alibi but he hadn't expected to drop the figure. Everything had changed now.

It was only as he approached the door of the club that he began to wonder if he could go on. He had to.

His hand still trembled as he began applying the blue-white makeup to his forehead.

"Holy Mother of God," he said aloud. "If I don't stop shaking I can't do tricks. I can't do cards."

He stood up and made a circle around the tiny dressing room, clutching his shaking fingers.

When he sat in front of the mirror again he was steadier.

Could he do it?

Just as he was finishing his red mouth, the door burst open.

The pale, freckled, frightened face of the call boy appeared.

"Bomb alert! Everybody out. NOW!"

The man called Calcularius slumped in his chair. He began to laugh as he smeared makeup with a steadier hand. He couldn't stop laughing. Nothing had gone right today and now he'd been saved by a bloody bomb.

LONG DAY'S JOURNEY INTO NIGHT Kim read on the marquee as the cab deposited them in front of the Abbey. "Why are they doing a play by an American? I thought the Abbey did only plays by Irish writers."

"O'Neill *is* an Irish writer, dear heart," Sydney answered. "From the Irish section of New London, Connecticut."

Laughing, they entered the theatre.

"How about one dark and one light chocolate?"

"Fine. I love the way everyone eats candy at plays over here."

They inspected the selection on the chocolate-laden island in the foyer.

"The other night at the Drury Lane I thought the crackling of the paper would be a distraction but I joined right in chewing away and didn't even notice."

"There's another custom at the Abbey you'll like. We order a drink now and pay for it, and then pick it up at the intermission—interval as they say—without having to stand in line at a crowded bar."

"If that's an example of Irish efficiency, I'm all for it."

"They are not noticeably efficient but they don't let anything interfere with getting a drink. It's the national sport. What will you have?"

"Irish coffee."

"Why not. And, I'll have Jameson's, neat, please." The smiling man behind the counter handed them their receipts.

The agent had delivered the good center stalls he promised. Kim was surprised by the sleek interior of the theatre.

"I was expecting something old with gilt cherubs."

"The old Abbey burned some years back. There are pictures of it up-stairs in the bar, and portraits of stars like Sara Allgood and Barry Fitzgerald. Be sure you look at them when we go up."

The house lights started to dim and the foots came up. Kim felt the shiver of terror that all actors remember at that moment.

"I'm just as glad I'm not on, aren't you?" Sydney whispered. "I can remember the applause but I can also remember the hollow feeling in my stomach the day of an opening."

The vacant seat beside them was presently filled to capacity by an enormous young man wearing rough denim work clothes, his feet shod in heavy brogans. Four rows ahead, a group of American tourists were loudly discussing their aching arches, trying to remember the names of castles they had visited and complaining about Irish food. They were still chattering when the curtain went up.

"Too long, but when wasn't O'Neill?" Sydney commented as they climbed the wide stairs to the bar. "Are you disappointed in the performance?"

"Heavens, no. I'm fascinated. It's much different than I expected. The acting is so—florid. I don't find it too long at all. Of course any theatre seems great to me. I haven't seen a whole lot lately."

"The Irish coffee section is down there. I'll pick up my drink and meet you in a second."

The room was modern with paneled walls and tiny spotlights in the ceiling Kim noticed as she seated herself on a low bench and took a sip. Abbey players of bygone days faced her from the wall opposite, all in heavy ancestor frames, each lighted separately. Kim pointed as Sydney joined her. "Isn't that Kevin McCarthy over there?"

"Where?"

"Over your left shoulder, look."

She leaned sideways to get a better view. "What do you know, it is. I wonder what he's doing here."

"In a play probably. Did you know he's Mary McCarthy's brother? I read it somewhere."

"Really. That's the trivia for the day."

Kim's attention was suddenly focused on a man whose profile was silhouetted in one of the overhead lights.

"Who is that devastating man? Certainly he must be an actor, but he doesn't look Irish."

"Which one? I see several who are rather dazzling."

"That one turning toward us. He's beautiful. Like Marcello Mastroianni. Or is it Tony Curtis in an old movie?"

"You must see a lot of old films to choose those two examples. You turn everyone into a movie star, don't you. If I didn't know better I'd say you're stage struck."

"Do you know him?" She ignored Sydney's teasing. "He's looking at you."

Sydney peered through the crowd. "Walter Carrasco."

In two quick strides he was beside them, smiling at Kim and embracing Sydney enthusiastically. He actually clicked his heels and bowed from the waist. Kim thought he was going to kiss her hand. Hoped he was. But he didn't. Walter Carrasco was slim with a wide-shouldered muscular body, appearing to be taller than he really was. His hair was black and wavy, eyes so dark they seemed opaque. His glance gave off sparks.

"Whatever are you doing here?"

He shrugged and flashed a smile. "What are *you*?"

"I'm here about some curtains. And it's Kim's first time in Ireland so we're doing the tourist bit too."

"If you have some free time let me show you and the beautiful Kim a little of Italy in Ireland," he invited.

Kim blushed at his obvious admiration and found him extremely charming.

"When? We've been just standing around waiting for a handsome man to invite us out."

Italy in Ireland? Where on earth? Kim envisioned red checked tablecloths, candles in Chianti bottles and a smiling *mamma mia* serving pasta.

"Where are you staying?"

"At the Shelbourne, as usual."

"I'll pick you up at noon. We'll start with lunch."

"Italian food?" Sydney laughed.

"No," Walter replied, "Italy comes later."

The lights dimmed and the bar crowd moved toward the stairs. Kim expected him to invite them for a drink after the play and was disappointed when he left with a casual, "See you at noon."

"Who is he?" she whispered as the house went dark.

Sydney's reply was intriguingly vague. She had done a decorating job for his boss.

It was a beautiful night after the rain and they walked slowly past Trinity and along Grafton Street discussing the play and the Abbey players.

"Would you like a nightcap?"

"Heavens! I've done nothing but drink since I've been with you. What I'd really like is a black and white soda."

"You're in the right town for that too. There's a place near here still open."

As Kim drank her soda she brought up Walter.

"What does that glorious man do? Is he an actor?"

Sydney hesitated just long enough. "He's a gangster."

"A what?" Kim choked on the ice cream.

"A gangster. You know, like on television."

"How do you know?"

"If I gave you his boss's name you'd shudder. He's one of the most infamous Mafia types in the States."

Kim shuddered. "How do you know?"

"I told you, I did a decorating job for him. He took one of those glass apartments on the East River with astronomical rents and no charm, and wanted me to do something with it. He was referred by a friend—a staid Wall Street type. He was surrounded by boys like Walter and they couldn't have been nicer. The place was a dream when I finished," she added.

"Walter's mad about you," Kim observed. "I can tell by the way he looks."

"He likes older women," Sydney bantered. "I probably remind him of his mother." But a faint color crept into her cheeks.

Kim laughed. "Yes, his mother. I'll bet you had an affair with him."

"Of sorts."

"How can you get involved with gangsters? Work for them? Sleep with them?" Kim savored both possibilities.

"I guess I'm a little dishonest, luv."

Kim looked at her in astonishment. "You can't be a *little* dishonest. Either you are honest or you aren't."

"That belief is one of your most charming. You're still such a child. So protected. By your parents first. Then by Scott, I suppose. You don't come up against the real problems that make life complicated. In my business I see dishonesty in a dozen ways. I try to avoid it myself but...." She broke off. "Nothing is black or white, ever, luv. Even that soda, now it's all cafe au lait. Let's make for home. I'm meeting the weavers at nine o'clock."

13 When Kim looked at her travel clock she realized she had slept soundly for almost eight hours. Maybe it was the unfamiliar dampness, the foggy atmosphere that made her hair curl and her eyes heavy. She felt sleepy even in the daytime. She had been dreaming, a complicated involved dream in which she had lost something. It seemed essential that she find out what it was. She concentrated hard but when she heard the shower running she knew Sydney would soon come to wake her. And then she dozed.

A few moments later, phone in hand, Sydney had to ask her twice to find out if she wanted anything extra for breakfast.

"What's the matter with you this morning? Are you hung over from that black and white soda?"

"I don't know. I feel strange and a little sickly."

"All that candy we had at the Abbey. You have a chocolate hangover. You'll feel better after some strong tea."

"Maybe." Kim shook her head to clear it. "I know I've been dreaming but I can't remember. All I know for sure is that I was a little girl again. It was the kind of dream where you know you've lost something but you don't know what it is. You search and search and never find it. No wonder I'm tired."

"Perfectly natural," Sydney remarked airily. "You're in Ireland and your ancestors were Irish so you're Irish too. The little people have taken something from you. Who was it came from around Dublin, your great-grand-mother?"

"My great-great-grandmother. My grandmother used to tell me about her when I was little."

"Maybe she has a message for you."

"Oh Sydney," Kim laughed uneasily.

"Well, I'm glad you're finally awake. I wish I could be still dreaming but I've got to get going. You explore Dublin a bit and let's meet at Brown Thomas a little after eleven. Here's a map. It's easy to find your way around."

Kim chose a green polka-dot shirt and white pants but put on sneakers for her walk. She strolled, enjoying the fine morning. Housewives chatted on neat doorsteps. Incredibly rosy-cheeked fat babies were out for airings in their prams.

She walked through the handsome facade of Trinity College and felt she was in another world as she crossed the wide square looking for the library. After she had viewed the *Book of Kells* and returned to the quad-rangle she sat on a bench admiring the ancient buildings. No one even glanced at her and she felt as if she were invisible. The strange, disoriented feeling she had on waking persisted. It was almost eleven when she found herself at the department store where she was to meet Sydney.

It was then that she began to understand the dream. She was a small child back in her grandmother's house. She was in the dining room and there was a corner china closet, all rounded glass, with shelves holding a clutter of bric-a-brac. One piece in particular was her favorite, a ceramic Bo-Peep dressed in pink with a tiny lamb at her feet. Her grandmother used to unlock the cabinet and let her cradle the shepherdess in her lap. She remembered Gram telling her stories her own grandmother had told about the Old Country where the figure had come from, but she was sleepy and soon she would be put on a big brass bed and covered with a down quilt incredibly soft and warm.

And now, in Brown Thomas, she was standing again in front of a glass-fronted cabinet. In it, this time dressed in blue but almost a twin of that one long ago, was a shepherdess. She stood about eight inches high and had incredible tiny perfect flowers trailing across her pale skirt, falling in a heap at her wee feet. One delicate hand held a slender staff and a half-smile played about her lips as if she was not too worried about her sheep.

"Isn't she a dear?"

A grey-haired woman had come up beside Kim as she stood locked in thought.

"Would you like to see her alone? She's Meissen, you know."

"Oh, may I?"

The woman unlocked the case, placing the figure on a handsome eighteenth century table for her to admire. She walked away to let Kim enjoy it.

She entirely forgot where she was, thinking back sadly to those days long ago and how little she knew her grandmother. How she wished she had listened to those tales.

"When I suggested we meet at Brown Thomas I never thought I'd find you in the antique section," she heard Sydney saying. "It's almost eleven-thirty. We need to meet Walter in a few minutes."

"Look," Kim said excitedly. "It's Meissen. And old. Isn't she wonderful?" She upended the figure and showed Sydney the price tag. "Only a hundred pounds, is that possible?"

The saleswoman, who had returned just as Sydney came in, reminded them that, as it was an antique, there was no duty.

"Also, no insurance," Sydney remarked.

"You see, when an object is old it is considered irreplaceable and we cannot insure it."

Sydney picked up the figure with great care and examined each intricate flower across the skirt and at the feet.

The clerk seemed genuinely pleased that the American girl loved one of her treasures. She assured them that it could be packed to travel safely.

"We do it often," she said. "The chaps downstairs put it first in cotton wool and then tissue, and finally in a box with packing materials so it will not move a trifle."

"Where did you find it?" Sydney asked. "It appears to be genuine. Ones that old and in such good condition are scarce now." She returned the figure to the table.

"Oh, indeed, yes, it is. We will give the lady a statement that it is genuine and at least one hundred sixty years old. It came from an estate in Wexford, recently settled. And this desk also." She gestured to an elaborately inlaid *escritoire* that Sydney and Kim moved over to inspect.

"Are you sure you have the patience to carry it?" Sydney asked in a low voice. "It is a good buy, and if you really want it so much—I never think of you as the antique type, somehow."

Kim started to tell her about her grandmother and the Bo-Peep and when she was a little girl but Sydney was looking at her watch again and wondering if they'd have time to change.

The clerk was back in a few moments with the shepherdess in a box neatly wrapped in brown paper and tied with strong twine. It made a handy package, about the size of a shoe box, and Kim was reassured that it would be no problem to carry.

Their cab stopped behind a dark green Jaguar parked in front of the Shelbourne.

"I expect that's our hero," Sydney said. "I won't have time to freshen my makeup and change into my new dress."

"You look marvelous as always," Kim protested. "I think you invented high fashion."

"Thanks, dear heart, but it takes longer and longer to look the way I once did."

Walter came down the steps, himself quite a sight in a pale summer suit, button-down avocado and brown shirt with lots of collar and cuffs showing. Kim thought again that he should have been an actor. She excused herself to leave the shepherdess in safety.

While she was upstairs Sydney told Walter about the department store antique.

"I'd like to see it. You know Mamma collects figurines."

"How is Mamma? You haven't mentioned her today."

"I haven't had a chance. I just got here. She's fine." He grinned.

It was a long-standing joke between them that Walter had the Latin devotion to his mother and talked about her frequently.

The restaurant was new and small and chic.

"I don't know this place." Sydney looked around. "I like it though."

"It's been here only a few months."

"You must come to Dublin often to have discovered it."

"Fairly often."

Kim looked around the room as Walter ordered drinks. She was astonished by the youth of the waiters. "They couldn't be out of school yet."

Sydney and Walter laughed.

"First place," Sydney said, "they're not all waiters. Lots of them are still apprentices."

"These boys will never see high school. They've been working since they were little kids. It takes years to get to be waiters. Their teachers are the chefs in the kitchen."

"Those little fellows at the hotel, the pages. Don't they go to school?"

"Sometimes they go, I suppose, but their families need the wages and the tips," Walter explained.

Kim looked distressed. "But they're so little to be working."

Sydney shook her head. "The same dear Kim. Always worrying about folks. Can you believe, when she was little, she put her allowance in parking meters that had expired. Luv, those moppets at the hotel are the lucky ones. They have jobs."

Lunch was magnificent. Sole and fresh asparagus. For dessert Walter had ordered a fine champagne.

"This is very pleasant," Sydney remarked. "So restful after those damn weavers. You know, when I got to the shop this morning one of them had the bright idea of putting purple in the design where we had especially used a sample of the client's blue. It was to pick up the blue in her carpet—a fabulous lush chenille, cost a fortune. And this clown thinks purple would be more interesting. Every time I hire these local craftsmen I know I'm in for something cataclysmic before the job is done. But handwoven curtains are all the rage now."

The day was perfect and Walter opened the sun roof to the blue, cloudless sky. He maneuvered skillfully through Dublin traffic into the countryside beyond.

"The natives call this cove the Bay of Naples. You'll see why." He parked the car at the edge of the cliffs of Killiney.

They got out to look down. Sydney in the rear. The scene was indeed Mediterranean. Pastel villas with red tile roofs were scattered in a profusion of roses and dark green shrubbery. Houses with names like "Capri" and "Sorrento" were severely locked behind wrought iron gates. At the foot of the steep incline far, far below, waves washed onto a sandy beach. Sea gulls wheeled and swooped over the sailboats dancing in the sun. Beyond the jetty a white packet boat was coming in.

"That's the steamer to Dun Laoghaire," Sydney said. "I took it from Liverpool once, just for fun. We docked in the middle of the night and there was no connection to town. And freezing cold."

"It's hard to imagine you without a man meeting the boat," Walter remarked. "Where were all your admirers?"

They exchanged looks and Kim wondered what was between them. Just a decorating job for his boss? Or maybe a romance? Or, was the boss the romance? She strolled down a lane to get a better view of the bay.

Walter put his arms around Sydney. "Why don't we play a little joke on Kim?" he whispered. "We'll tell her that the page boys at the Shelbourne are really midgets and they're all about forty."

Sydney giggled. "You know how she is. She'd go up to them and ask if they're married, how many children they have, what are their wages."

For an instant they smiled at one another conspiratorially.

"Oh, Walter, you're impossible! You bring out the very worst side of my nature. Stop it this minute."

Walter drove very fast but with skill and in no time they were in front of the Shelbourne.

"I wish I could take you to dinner but I have to drive up to Belfast," he said as he kissed Sydney's lips and Kim's hand. "Hope I'll get to see you in New York," he called from the car. "Where do you stay?"

"The Bellamy." She started to explain why she stayed there but decided he wouldn't care. "Oh, yes, I hope to see you too."

She wondered exactly where and how their paths might cross in New York. Did he intend to call her? Did she know anyone who would know a person like Walter? Well, Sydney, of course. But then perhaps interior decorating was like the theatre. It was an umbrella which sheltered all types. She also wondered what her mother would say, or worse still, her father. The thought of her father and Walter in the same room brought a smile to her lips.

"Why's he going to Belfast?" Kim asked as they watched him drive away.

"I haven't the vaguest."

"What's he doing in Ireland anyhow?"

"I don't know, dear heart. Maybe he had a horse he wanted to see run or maybe he likes Irish girls. Perhaps an errand."

"Or maybe he's involved in the riots up there, or maybe he came to kill someone," Kim goaded her.

Sydney opened her eyes wide and shrugged. "Maybe."

14

"Let me warn you," Ian was saying in the Shelbourne lobby two hours later. "Night life in Dublin is different from other cities."

"Not all the night clubs, girly shows, bright lights," remarked Sydney. "But there's lots going on. You'll see."

Holding Kim's raincoat so she could slip it on, Henry commented, "It's far more memorable in the long run than most Saturday nights." He turned down her collar and brushed her cheek affectionately.

"I expect it's no change for you," Ian interjected. "I rather imagine Saturday nights in Edinburgh are much the same. Or are you raising all kinds of hell up there?"

Was it Kim's imagination, or was Ian condescending when he spoke directly to Henry? She had felt on other occasions that he might be.

"It's mainly pub crawling," Ian went on. "But in Dublin that has many interesting facets."

The sunny afternoon had been followed by a sudden downpour. It had subsided and now the rain fell gently, hinting that it might soon become mist. Henry opened his umbrella and held it over Kim protectively as they walked toward Grafton Street. She wondered how she would feel when she saw him tonight. Would they both be uncomfortable? She felt safe and happy and completely at ease as she tucked her arm around his.

"What have you two been doing since you arrived in Dublin?"

Kim thought what a sincere ring Henry's voice always had, as if he really wanted to know.

What a fatuous question, Sydney thought. "The whole tourist bit. The Abbey, first of all."

"We saw *Long Day's Journey Into Night.*"

"How was it?"

"Long," Sydney replied.

"I loved it," Kim protested. "And I was thrilled over being there. I've dreamed of seeing the Abbey Players ever since I was in school. I had Irish coffee during the interval. I remembered the proper term and didn't call it intermission."

She went along enthusiastically describing the play, the patrons, the bar and the portraits, making both men feel that the Abbey must be far more exciting than they remembered.

"I saw a page of the *Book of Kells.*" Kim continued her travelogue. "I must confess I was disappointed. I was naive enough to think that I could see the whole book and maybe even turn the pages and gasp over the illustrations."

Henry smiled at her indulgently. "Most everyone has that idea. I did too, years ago."

"But it's fascinating that they turn a page every day. If you lived here you could go often and see lots of pages."

"Let's just duck in here and have a little drink." Ian led the way down wide stone steps and through a low doorway. The room was Georgian, or pseudo-Georgian, and at this hour almost empty. "We're a little early, but let's enjoy one quiet drink before all the places are packed." He guided them to a cozy corner table. It was an elegant place and Kim hoped they might linger for a while, but Ian was already planning their next stop. He seemed restless.

Kim and Henry were ahead and had reached the sidewalk when they heard Ian's voice roughly order someone away. "No, no, not now, old chap!"

They both turned. A slim youngish man stood on the steps beside Sydney and Ian. A soggy dark wool cap was pulled low almost to his eyes.

His macintosh collar was turned up but the coat was open to the waist and the black sweater under it was wet too, as if he had been standing in the rain for a long while. In the dim light of the doorway he appeared more frightened than frightening.

Ian guided Sydney swiftly up the stairs. The man looked after them angrily.

"What happened?" Kim asked.

"Just an unpleasant fellow unhappy with the world," Ian assured her as they began to walk quickly away. "So sorry for the incident."

"You used not to have that sort of thing in Dublin," Henry commented, looking over his shoulder.

"He said you've got to help me, or something of the sort," Sydney said. Her voice sounded strange. "He almost whispered so I could hardly hear. Oughtn't we have tried to do something?"

"Nonsense." Ian was irritated. Then his tone lightened. "Sometimes you surprise me, darling. These drunks are everywhere on a Saturday night. You can't help them all and you know the Irish, they can make up such a good tale of woe that I'd almost believe it myself."

Henry agreed.

"Now, where shall we have dinner?" Ian was the perfect host again. "Does Italian food appeal to you?"

"Or Chinese, or East Indian, or German?" Henry asked. "You'll find us very cosmopolitan."

"Or even Irish," Sydney laughed.

Both Ian and Henry had been callous about the stranger and now even Sydney was her gay self once more. Kim was upset by anyone in trouble and the perfection of the evening was marred. She did not readily join in the conversation.

They were walking past Brown Thomas. "You won't believe what Kim bought this morning. In this very store." She motioned to the darkened windows. "An antique."

"Or a reproduction alleged to be an antique," Ian suggested.

"No, I think it's authentic. They're very reliable. It was from an estate near Wexford. You know they have some lovely things but no one thinks of looking here for antiques."

Both men showed great interest in the shepherdess and Kim was flattered. Ian said the best Meissen was getting rare and would command attractive prices one day. He assumed that she had bought it as an investment.

"Oh, I'd never sell it. I didn't buy it because it might become valuable. It reminded me...of something," she broke off lamely. She thought he might laugh if she told them about her grandmother. She could almost hear Sydney teasing, 'Everyone has grandmothers; one just doesn't talk about them.' She found herself telling how big the shepherdess was and how carefully the store packed and tied it up in brown paper and strong twine. Suddenly she laughed at herself.

"Here I am telling *you people* about antiques."

Ian assured her they were genuinely interested, and Kim was again impressed by his smoothness and charm. Always able to make everyone feel at ease, and yet he made her uneasy.

Last Saturday night, eating a quiet dinner alone in Florence, Kim had not imagined that in one week's time she would be walking down a Dublin street in a misty rain with Sydney and two attractive men. Scott would like Henry James. He would not like Ian Hardwicke, she decided. Why? She was not quite certain because she liked him rather a lot herself. The other night in London while dancing with him she had felt a giddy breathless thrill. Tonight when they came down into the lobby and the two men were waiting, she looked first at Ian and her heart actually beat faster. Strange though. She suddenly realized the feeling had been more akin to nervousness than excitement.

How utterly ridiculous. Why should she care what Scott thought of either of them?

Why didn't her heart beat faster at sight of Henry? He had been plenty exciting in the grass beside the Thames. She was glad it was not very light. She knew she was blushing just remembering the policeman signaling to move on.

Meanwhile, the others had decided on Italian food and Ian was asking if she agreed.

"Of course."

"You're very quiet." Henry sounded concerned.

"She's too weak from hunger to carry on a conversation," Sydney said. "At least *I'm* starving."

Ian smiled to himself as he led the way. She's just the girl we need, he decided.

"Oh look, there's Calcularius."

"Where?" Ian was startled.

"A picture of him there. In front of that club." Kim pointed to the conjurer almost life-size in makeup and costume.

"He goes back and forth between here and London. Very popular both places."

"And in Edinburgh as well," Henry added.

"Shall we go in?" Kim asked.

"No," Sydney said and walked on.

They had a couple of drinks before they ordered and Ian carefully selected wine, politely consulting them before he made a choice.

"Everyone seems so intense." Kim looked around. "What do you suppose they're discussing?"

"Politics," Ian suggested.

"The last race at Leopardstown," Sydney supplied.

"Religion," Henry speculated. "It's very big here you know, and almost anywhere you can hear interminable religious arguments."

"If you stay in Ireland long, luv, you have to declare yourself as either Catholic or Protestant."

"You mean people ask which you are?"

"Well, all but. The Irish are too polite to ask point blank. Like everything else, they talk around it, but they're not comfortable until they know."

"Can't you be an atheist and refuse to join either camp?"

"Not in Ireland," Henry laughed. "You're either a Catholic or a Protestant atheist."

"It's too complicated for me but I find it all delightful."

"After dinner, where?" Ian wanted to know. Kim had hoped they might just sit for a while. Her head was spinning after the wine and two, or was it three, drinks.

"Neary's," Henry suggested.

"Indeed." Ian's agreement was enthusiastic. "It's theatrical so you two will like it."

And after Neary's there was a place for literary types, and for newspaper types, and one that appeared to have appeal for all.

Kim was feeling woozy and not finishing her drinks but the others didn't appear to notice. By this time Ian and Sydney were having an hilarious time, and even solicitous Henry swept her along with them, not paying much attention to her withdrawal.

Later, as they were entering a nameless little snug beside Ha'penny Bridge, Kim stopped abruptly.

"Sydney, that was Walter!"

"What? Where?"

"Walter. Getting into a taxi." A square, black cab jerked away from the curb. "I thought he was in Belfast."

"He is. You're mistaken."

"Who's Walter?" Ian wanted to know.

"A friend we ran into at the Abbey. He was going to drive up to Belfast."

"He must have changed his mind," Henry said matter-of-factly.

"A woman's prerogative they say, but men do it too," Ian said.

They had just ordered drinks when the barman pleaded, "Time now, gentlemen, please."

No one appeared to hear him, but patrons leaned a little closer to one another and there was a busy scurrying to the bar for additional orders.

A moment later the blinds were drawn and conversation became hushed. The place had well worn benches and wooden tables. The bartender moved these closer together as he swabbed them down with a dingy rag. On each table was a collection box with the words, HELP THE AFRICAN MISSIONS. Kim put a few coins in one while Ian watched her cynically. The men had ordered pints of stout. Sydney and Kim each had a glass of ale. A few customers left but others slipped in quietly to take their places in the dim room. Elbow to elbow, they sat with the locals for an hour or more of concentrated illegal drinking.

"I think it was the most nervous-making hour I've ever spent," Kim said a little thickly as they were approaching the hotel. "But it seemed so exciting."

"There are few illicit pleasures to equal after-hours drinking in Ireland if one has good companions," Ian commented.

"Look!" Kim exclaimed, just as they were about to enter the hotel. "Henry, that man over there"

His hand tightened on her arm. "Where?"

"The one who asked us for help. He's standing by that tall tree across the street."

The other three strained their eyes, peering out from the brightly lighted hotel facade into the shadowy park.

"You're sloshed, luv," Sydney said at last. "There's no one over there."

"There *is*."

They all looked at her in surprise.

"Kim, you're seeing things. There will be little men in green suits sitting on toadstools next," Sydney teased.

Ian studied Kim's face for a second before he proffered, "Why don't you insist that we come up for a last drink?"

He was obviously trying to divert her attention.

"Jesus, that's all we need," Sydney complained and invited them up.

"May we see your department store antique?" Ian asked as Sydney was pouring drinks from her flask.

Somewhat reluctantly she unlocked her suitcase.

Ian took the parcel from her, weighed it in his hands, and was thinking of cutting the twine with his knife. At that moment Sydney set one of the glasses too close to the edge of the table and Henry's sleeve brushed against it. The glass shattered and its contents splashed across the table.

"Oh, sorry, here, let me fix that." Henry was on his feet running for a towel. He carefully picked up the pieces of glass while Sydney poured another drink.

Kim grabbed her package and placed it out of the way.

When they had cleaned up the mess, Ian seemed to have forgotten all about the shepherdess. She was just as glad she didn't have to share her treasure. While they were talking she put it back in the suitcase, compelled to look across the street to St. Stephen's Green as she passed the window.

As soon as Henry and Ian left she began to talk about the strange frightened man.

"To bed with you," Sydney said firmly, switching off lamps. "You won't be able to lift your head in the morning."

"Sydney, we should have tried to help him. You were worried too. I could tell by the way your voice sounded."

"The men were right. It's like the beggars in Mexico. You can't help them all so why let one break your heart. What could we have done? He was a nut of some kind, one of the rioters, perhaps. There are plenty of fanatics left in Ireland."

The lights were soon all out and it was quiet and cool. Kim lay awake for a long time. Her head was beginning to ache and when she closed her eyes the room spun. She tried to count the drinks and the places they had gone but gave up after about four.

She *had* seen the man standing on the edge of St. Stephen's Green. Of that she was certain. And Walter? She wanted to ask why he hadn't gone to Belfast but Sydney would try to convince her that he had. The poor man was so desperate. He wasn't an ordinary drunk and his clothes were respectable. He didn't look like a beggar. If she had insisted, Henry might have done something even if the others laughed at her. She felt spooky and shivered in the darkness, wishing the door had a better lock.

15

"What was that scene with Danny all about?"

They were cutting across St. Stephen's Green. Both knew the reason for choosing that circuitous route to their hotel.

"I don't know but I intend to find out."

"Do you think Kim really saw him in the Green?"

"Possibly. I saw him again when we came out after dinner. He's somewhere lurking about. I'll wait until he turns up."

"What's he thinking of, accosting us that way? Suppose the girls...."

"My God," Ian cut in, "I've never been so shocked in my life. We started up the steps and Danny jumped out just in front of us. I damn near called him by name. He's likely been spying on us all night."

"How did he know where to find you?"

"He knows the restaurants I visit. He has delivered messages to me several times at one place or another."

"Kim thinks Danny—of course she calls him Calcularius— doesn't like you, or is afraid of you."

"What caused her to think that?"

"Intuition, she said. When he joined us after the performance she felt he didn't want to be near you."

"If he's botched it, she's right. He should be afraid."

"Do you think something's gone wrong?"

"Nothing too serious, I think, or he'd have gotten in touch with me earlier."

They paused for a moment on the bridge and peered into the darkness. There was no sign of Danny O'Rahilly.

"Why don't you go along," Ian suggested. "No need for us both to stay. I'll see what the trouble is."

"Are you certain I shouldn't stay?"

"No point in it."

"Well, you know the fellow better than I. I trust your handling him. Rap on my door when you come in."

Henry was relieved to escape a confrontation. After all, Danny worked for Ian. It was his problem. Ian said that he had been extremely useful in a couple of instances but Henry knew little of the details of his involvement. Didn't care to know.

Ian paced from the bridge to the edge of the duck pond and back again, waiting impatiently. Ten minutes went by, and he began to think Danny was not there. Then there was a movement behind a bush and a voice whispered, "Mister Hardwicke."

"Don't call me by name. Not ever again." Ian's voice was low and cold. He had made few mistakes in his professional life and letting Danny know his identity was certainly one of them. He was haunted by the knowledge that this man could identify him. No time to think about that now. He got on with the business at hand.

"What's wrong with you? Do you have the object?"

"Sure, but there was a fuss. A terrible fuss."

For a moment Ian stared at him, not comprehending. Then he grabbed the front of his bulky sweater. The wet wool slipped through his gloves and he tightened his grasp.

"What kind of fuss? Speak up." He shook Danny roughly.

Some of Danny's actor's cockiness came back. "Don't you be making like gentry with me. I know you for what you really are. You're no better than me."

Ian released him with an oath and Danny stepped back.

"All right, all right, what happened?"

"Holy Mother of God, I pushed him on the stair and he must have tripped. He was old. I didn't shove hard, I swear I didn't. I don't *know* what happened."

"Pushed who, for Christ sake?" Ian tried to be calm but his voice was hoarse.

A pair of lovers strolled toward them on the dim path, their arms locked tightly, voices low and tender. Ian and Danny stood very still in the shadows of a clump of bushes. Each could hear the other's breathing as they waited.

"Whom did you push?"

"It was the end of the day and the place was empty. The alarm didn't sound, just like you said. There was no one there. I started down the steps. All of a sudden I heard something. It sounded like someone was coming up so I waited. He got right up to me and I had to do something, didn't I? He was old but he was big and he moved pretty good. I had a stocking over my face so he couldn't tell who it was. He couldn't catch me if I got past him. I didn't want to hurt him, but he was blocking the way. I just pushed him aside, see, so I could get by. He fell against the wall and missed his footing."

"Then what?"

"I found out he was dead."

"Dead!"

Danny's voice rose hysterically, even higher than his usual falsetto. "I didn't even know he was hurt until I saw the paper. Said there would be an investigation." Danny's shoulders heaved. He was shivering in his wet clothes.

"You idiot," Ian hissed. "You bloody blundering fool! Give me the key."

Danny backed away and straightened up. "I'll be taking the money first. Now." He looked around. "I've got to get away."

"Have you ever had difficulty collecting from me? I shouldn't pay you this time. You know what you were hired to do. How in heaven's name were you so careless as to kill a man?"

"I told you, it was an accident."

"The key."

With an almost imperceptible movement Danny started to reach for an inside coat pocket. He thought better of it. "The money first. And, I'll need an extra five thousand pounds."

"You'll get the ten thousand agreed upon and if you're wise, you will be on the first aircraft to the States tomorrow."

"You know I can't. I have to go to London to get the papers. You promised. You know that's why I agreed to do this. I think you'll do well to give me the extra money. I can identify you. I'll drag you into this before I'll hang for murder." Danny was aware that Ian was vulnerable.

Ian too was well aware.

"All right, come along, let's get the parcel and I'll give you the money." Ian started to walk away.

"Now? You'll have the key. Get it tomorrow. That was the plan."

"You've changed the plan by your bungling."

Danny stood still for a minute and then followed him.

They began the walk through dark streets in the direction of the Liffey to the bus station beyond the Customs House where the package was checked.

Ian Hardwicke was a success because he made quick, unemotional decisions. Here he was in the most important single transaction he had ever attempted and a blundering small-time magician was not going to ruin things. Ian himself had become momentarily disconcerted when he learned that delivery was to be made in New York, but he recovered almost at once. It was unfortunate that this accident had occurred, but he assayed its consequences and the matter was settled in his mind.

"I think I recall a passage just about here that comes out on the river," Ian said. "Saves going the long way round."

"I know where you mean. Down to the right a bit, though," and O'Rahilly led the way.

Hardwicke glanced over his shoulder. The street was empty behind them as they entered the narrow passage between dark buildings. He looked beyond Danny to the black waters of the Liffey at the end of the dim opening. His hand shook ever so slightly as he squeezed the trigger. There was the soft THOP of the silenced revolver and Danny O'Rahilly began to slump. He twisted around and his arm shot up, clutching at the brick wall. For an instant his unbelieving eyes fixed on Ian. Then he settled slowly onto the damp cobbles in a heap. Remembering where Danny's hand had started to reach at mention of the key, Ian felt quickly for the man's inside coat pocket. He went through the other pockets. A few folded bank notes. The chap was bright enough, no identification. There was no need to check for signs of life. The range made it certain that Danny was not alive. Not looking back, he walked without haste toward the Liffey.

He had carried that small revolver for a long time, an accessory to a part of his business. This was the first time he had used it and he was surprised at how little emotion he felt. He sighed and thought if a man were obliged to engage in commerce he had to overlook certain deeds that went against the grain.

Henry James opened the door of his room when he head footsteps in the hall.

"Ah, it's you. Where've you been? I was getting nervous."

Ian followed him into the room. He placed the newspaper-wrapped parcel on the bed. "A million pounds, that." He sighed and sank into a chair.

"Here? Now?" Henry looked at the parcel with distaste. He had expected Ian would pick it up tomorrow. He would then quickly authenticate it and his personal implication would be minimal. Now he was shocked by the impact of having it here in his room."Weren't you to get it tomorrow?"

"Yes, but after I talked to Danny I thought it better to not wait." He looked around the room. "Have you got a drink? The dampness." He passed a hand over his eyes.

Henry produced a silver flask from his bag. "Whatever was his trouble? I was afraid he hadn't got it."

"He'd got it all right. Hard to believe but he's mixed up in some damn political ruckus."

"The Catholic riots I thought that was up north mostly."

"They've had trouble here too, you know."

"You have always claimed that Danny is a simple personality. A harmless actor with great dexterity and agility. How could you take a chance on anybody political?"

"I didn't know he was political when I first used him. I knew he was a thief and that was an important bit of information. Did I ever tell you how I knew that?"

"No."

"The first time I saw him was in a little place in Cork City. He was pretty good at sleight of hand even then. The bloody bum took my watch. I missed it and accused him. He panicked and returned it. I didn't turn him over but I always knew I could go to him when I needed his special skills. He had a brush or two with the police over the years. He fancied himself a cat burglar and did some time for getting caught removing jewelry from a flat via a second-story window. That's why this caper is so important to him. He needs papers and the money so he can go to New York and, as he imagines, go bigtime. He claims this is his last job of the sort. Perhaps it is. At any rate, I didn't know he was political, but you never know about the Irish."

They looked at each other and Ian shrugged.

"What explanation did he give for speaking to you in the street?"

"Says he's frightened." Ian took a thoughtful swallow of the whiskey. "Thinks they're going to kill him. Don't ask me who 'they' are. He wanted to get his payment and get out of town. I decided it was best. He's dangerous to us in this frame of mind."

Ian wished it were as simple as he was making it sound. He relaxed a little sipping his drink as his eyes focused on the object on the bed. An idea had occurred to him earlier when Kim showed them her package. Now he was sure he had been right.

"James, what does that parcel on the bed bring to mind?"

"A great art treasure about to be hidden away," Henry pronounced morosely. "And it brings fear to my mind. And guilt." He picked up the object for a moment and then laid it back on the bed. "And money," he added resignedly.

"Oh my God. Don't give me an editorial. Just tell me what it looks like." Henry was so pedantic sometimes.

"I don't know what it looks like. No games, it's after two o'clock, Hardwicke. What does it bring to mind?"

"The parcel Kim showed us. The one with her Meissen figure. This could easily be packed identically. I examined hers, checked it for size and weight. If we exchanged parcels she would do us a favor and never know it until she was safely in New York."

"I don't like it. You said Sydney would ask her to take it."

"Sydney hasn't asked her yet and we're running out of time. Kim's such a Girl Guide she doesn't know how to approach her."

"Enough of your condescending remarks about Kim. She happens to have a keen sense of morality, and since when is that a crime?"

"She really has reached you, hasn't she?"

"Yes, she has."

"My God, why didn't you just do it the other night instead of rolling around in the grass like an inept schoolboy? There are times when I think I haven't taught you a thing."

"And times when I think with regret that you have taught me far too much." He sighed. "Sydney says she will ask her. We can depend upon her, I think."

"You think. That's not good enough." Ian stood and still holding his glass, moved restlessly around the room. "No. The thing to do is duplicate her package."

"You should take it yourself. I said so when New York came up."

"Don't be a fool. We've gone over this. I can't be identified. When this sale is accomplished I can relax. I don't like doing this sort of thing any more than you do but I need the capital for the big legitimate art money. Do you think I want to be in the underground art market all my life? One slip on the wrong side of the law and I go down. I'd have to leave London forever. I'd end my days selling fake icons to tourists on street corners in Dubrovnik."

Henry laughed.

Ian failed to see the humor. "You take it."

"I wouldn't deliver it for any amount of money. It doesn't mean that much to me."

Ian knew Henry was a rock in certain areas. Besides, he rather relished the cleverness of getting Kim to take it without knowing she'd been, in her eyes, bad. "Then we're back where we started aren't we, Kimberleigh Brennan?"

"Why not be honest for once? *Ask* her to take it."

"You ask her," Ian snapped. "She's your girlfriend."

"I wish she were."

"You wish she were," Ian mocked him. "You always wait around wishing for things, don't you. Take them."

"I wanted to marry someone like her once. I was so poor it seemed hopeless," Henry went on in the same mood. "Not long after Trinity. I couldn't marry then with no prospects. Of course she married someone else. Since then I've drifted. But Kim...."

Ian was not listening.

"Why haven't you ever married? You could afford it."

Ian looked at him steadily before he answered.

"Primogeniture, old man," he said bleakly. "The curse of my class. I could have married, that's true, but what would I give to my heirs? Andrew has it all, the title, the land, the town house, what money was left after taxes. It's all been easy enough for you. You came from nothing so you didn't expect anything. You've made yourself a life, that's true. All very admirable. With a good deal of help from me," he added.

"Why couldn't you do the same for yourself? You could have gone to work just as I did. If you hadn't been so busy resenting your brother."

"Work? Work!" Ian expostulated, gesturing with his glass. "I wasn't brought up to work." He was getting a little drunk, finally.

"Heard the news, old boy? Times have changed. The war is history. *Noblesse oblige* is dead. Even gentlemen are taking jobs and glad to get them. With your polish you could push Bentleys."

Henry felt a touch spiteful and petty. Ian did not seem to care.

"The system's what's outdated, not gentlemen. Gentlemen are always needed in a civilized society. But the eldest inheriting the lot, that's what's wrong. The younger sons scrabbling for the crumbs. Look at all the great houses now and you'll see some dim bulb sitting on the land, raising his children to be presented at Court. And his younger brother, who has wits he never thought of, is clerking in The Temple or reading news on the telly. That's the fate we're doomed to."

Henry looked at him with interest.

"I always wondered what motivated you toward art. Certainly not love of it. Doesn't our causing this treasure to be banished make you feel guilty?"

"Certainly not. It's the reward I keep thinking of. If it's the real goods. If Danny hasn't tricked us."

"Goods!" snorted Henry.

Ian was on his feet, the thought impelling him. He ripped the newspaper away. He bent over the bed, looking at the object for a moment. Then he stepped back, executed a military half-turn and, with a flourish, bowed and said, "Herr Professor, if you will take over."

Henry James moved slowly to the bed. He held the bronze figure reverently and examined it carefully. He had researched it thoroughly. Danny had not tricked them. At last he said, "Your buyer is getting full value."

Ian smiled broadly and would have clapped him on the shoulder but Henry jerked away and walked to the window. He raised the sash and breathed deeply of the cool night air.

16

"It's yer breakfast coffee and the Irish Times, mum." Sydney, wearing a lace hankie on her head, bobbed a curtsey.

Kim staggered out of the bathroom. "Funny," she muttered.

"And a Bloody Mary," Sydney added, laughing when she saw Kim.

"Don't dare tell me you're not suffering."

"I am, but I'm the brave martyr type. I don't give in to hangovers."

Kim sat quietly sipping first one and then the other of the remedies. Sydney started at the back of the paper and acted out the comics, the society page and then the want ads with a clever mimicry that would have made her laugh if her head had not been throbbing.

"Do the race results interest you?"

"No, thanks."

"Let's skip the news. It's all bad." Sydney turned idly to the front page. "Jesus," she gasped. "Look at this."

Kim moved quickly to see where she was pointing and her head threatened to split. She grabbed it with both hands and held it tightly.

"That's the man who came up to us last night! Shot! Killed!"

This time it was Kim who was hesitant. "I don't think so. Who was he? When was he killed?"

Sydney ran a carefully manicured finger rapidly along the lines, taking in the facts. "Shot in the back. Sometime last night. Hasn't been identified yet."

Kim looked at the photograph on the front page. A body was lying on the ground and people were standing over it. He was wearing a coat like the man who had asked them for help and wet black hair fell over his still face. Newsprint blurred his features and it was hard to be sure.

"No, I don't think it's the same one," Kim said slowly. She didn't want to think so, or to admit if she did. If it was the same man, the one who asked for help, they might have saved him.

"Where was he killed?"

"Some place I never heard of."

"Do you know where it is? Near here?"

"Near the river, it says. I must be wrong. You don't seem to think it's the same person."

"I wasn't as close as you and Ian were. Ask him."

"But last night you recognized him across the street." Sydney glanced out the window toward the Green.

Before Kim could speak the telephone rang. They jumped.

"Hello," Sydney said. "Oh, it's you. Good morning. Yes, we are, sort of." She nodded as she listened. "Can we give Kim ten minutes? Fine." She turned to Kim. "Ian's downstairs. Henry will be along shortly. Ian and I will go in one car and you and Henry will take the other. They'll drive back here later and we'll go on to the airport and turn our car in there—okay?"

Kim tried to signal agreement without moving her head.

"Oh Lord, here we go again—the Rover Girls on tour. I'd better dash. Ian hates to be kept waiting. Hurry now. I'll send a man for the bags."

Kim stood up too suddenly and had to close her eyes as her head resisted the move and the room twirled.

"Oh, your poor head. Well, see you at Durrow House," Sydney said breezily as she left. Kim noticed she took the paper.

"So sorry to have to take two cars," Henry said when Kim joined him. "Ian refuses to use public transportation." He held the door of the green Ford for her. "Made him seem a hell of a fellow when we were at school, but after all these years a facade is a bit of a nuisance. He'll walk a hundred miles though, as you learned last night."

Henry did not seem himself. He was talking rapidly and at the same time seemed distracted. "How are you feeling?" he asked as he worked his way through city traffic.

"A little hung over," Kim admitted.

"It was a bit of a late night," he agreed. "I'm not in such fine shape myself. Hope we haven't spoiled Ireland for you."

"Oh, no. I'm just a little tired and sleepy but I'll be all right after a while."

Kim looked over at him and liked his profile—his nose slightly crooked, his high forehead and crisp reddish hair. He turned to her and smiled.

"I didn't have time to read the paper this morning," she said, hoping to appear casual. "Did you? Anything happen that we should know about?" She felt guilty as she watched him carefully. Did he hesitate before he answered? He sometimes did that anyhow, so it might mean nothing.

"No. I had trouble falling asleep. And then I had trouble getting out of bed this morning. I don't remember seeing a paper. Ian must have taken it."

Was Henry lying?

Was it the man who had asked them for help?

Did Henry know him?

Did Ian?

If one did, the other must.

Was it her imagination last night that he was in the park?

She couldn't be certain of anything except that her head was killing her. She sighed and hoped Henry didn't know. He let her sit without talking, enjoying the morning. The road out of Dublin crossed a lovely green panorama dotted with neat cottages, a vine-covered church and tiny, rock-fenced pastures blurred by morning mist. For a time the sea was beside them and then they left it to pass through a series of villages.

"I think you'll find the house of interest. The gardens are magnificent. As you can imagine, Ireland is perfect for gardens. There is great variety in the soil and the winters are fairly mild. Almost everything thrives here because it is so rainy. We Irish were so busy fighting among ourselves that gardens didn't become important until the eighteenth century.

"The house is pretty typical of big places where practical touches like modern plumbing and central heating were added a couple of hundred years after the structure was conceived. A bit slapdash but quite functional.

"The rococo plasterwork ceiling is exceptional. It dates from the eighteenth century too. In the 1730s a pair of Italian brothers were brought here to fashion a ceiling for one of the great houses. They were master plasterers who could create all sorts of intricate beasts and fruits and vines and flowers. The first thing you know, dozens of Irish artisans had learned the techniques and the result was ceilings like the one you'll see."

"I shall love the gardens, I know. I'd hoped to get out into the country-side around London and see some houses and gardens but I was on a merry-go-round the whole time."

"You and Sydney may wish to look briefly at Lord Harleigh's things but you will probably enjoy the house and grounds more."

"What's in the collection?"

"Several very important seventeenth and eighteenth century paintings and a number of minor ones, and a few pieces of sculpture. He is quite a collector, but fickle. He has now turned to Postimpressionists and is selling a few canvases to make space for his new treasures."

"Are you going to buy something?"

Henry looked at her with amusement. "You flatter me. I couldn't afford even the most modest piece. I'm here solely as a consultant. Ian plans to bid on several things and asked me to have a look. I wish you could be here for the auction itself; it is very exciting business."

"When is it?"

"The first week in September." He braked the car. "Sorry for the sudden halt. I nearly bypassed the lane. It's considered very grand not having a sign to mark the entrance." He cut sharply off the road and into a lane bounded by high stone fences. Recent rains had shifted the gravel and there were ruts so Henry had to drive carefully to avoid high centers.

"If he's so rich you'd think he'd pave the drive."

"That would be ostentatious."

The car park was neatly bordered by flower beds and shaded by old trees. The house was all turrets and battlements surrounded by a grassed-over moat. Sydney and Ian were standing in front of the door talking with their host.

Lord Harleigh was in his sixties, short, fat and bald. He insisted upon personally showing Sydney and Kim what he considered the most interesting rooms. Each plaster swirl of the famous ceiling intrigued him as it did them. He was kind and thoughtful, not at all pretentious, wearing a shabby tweed coat with elbow patches and walking with them at a leisurely pace through the rooms as if he had no other thought for the day.

After a time he led them to a gate and suggested the garden beside the lake as a pleasant beginning for their rambles.

"Ian convinced me it wasn't our boy in the paper," Sydney said as soon as they were alone. "I thought I'd better tell you so you can stop worrying. I know you. You have been going over and over it in your mind."

"Did you want to be convinced?"

"Well now, you've certainly changed. This morning early you thought I was mistaken."

"I don't know what I believe now."

"Think about it tomorrow, Scarlett. It's such a dear country we're in and you've seen only one facet of Ireland—Dublin." Sydney linked her arm through Kim's. "Let's enjoy the gardens."

They leaned against the balustrade and looked down a series of terraces of velvet grass. At the bottom of a long flight of steps two life-sized stone lions faced one another. On the small lake sculptured figures were sending spouts of water high into the air. There was a path sheltered by thick trees and they walked along slowly, remarking on the luxuriousness and variety of trees and shrubbery. There were acres of landscaped gardens, all exquisitely manicured. A gardener was performing light Sunday chores.

"I had no idea it would be this beautiful."

"Impressed?"

"Yes, but not just impressed by the grandeur of it. Imagine, all of this magnificence is a home, too. That nice Lord Harleigh lives here. It's a way of life I didn't know existed any longer."

"Oh, it still exists, but you will observe that he has to sell a Rembrandt or Vermeer now and again to support his pleasures."

Kim reached down and dangled her fingers in a fountain beside them. "I feel much better now. Seeing this wonderful place has been a tonic. I'll always remember it. I've almost forgotten about the—you know—the man in the paper"

After a couple of hours Ian and Henry found them back on the terrace still admiring the view.

Lord Harleigh was gracious and sincere as he invited them to stay for luncheon. Kim wished they could but Ian had made reservations at a nearby inn and then they must go their separate ways.

"Let me have the keys to the car you came down in," Ian said to Henry after they had savored a country feast. "We'll transfer Sydney's things." He walked with Sydney to the car. "I told you that you need not worry about getting that birthday gift to the States. Now I'll show you how I solved the problem."

He unlocked the boot and handed Sydney a package. "Have you seen this before?"

"Of course. It's Kim's shepherdess. Where did you get it?"

"No, darling, it is not. But an exact replica of the parcel. Rather clever of me, don't you agree?"

"Hm, ye-es, but what about the shepherdess?"

"You stow this in your luggage and switch packages later. Then take the shepherdess next week when you go over. Childishly simple, isn't it? It struck me when we saw the package."

"But I'm going to New York. I shan't be seeing Kim."

"You can certainly have the Meissen packed properly for shipping. Look, I'll arrange it for you so you don't bother."

"Wait, let me see if I understand all of this. We let Kim take *this* package thinking it is her shepherdess. I appreciate the beauty of not having to persuade her, believe me, but suppose she opens it?"

"Not a great chance that she will, do you think? After all, she's leaving tomorrow morning. If she opens it before she leaves you, I depend upon your ingenuity. Otherwise, you call her the moment she reaches New York and tell her the truth. After all, we haven't done anything so terrible. Involved her in a bit of petty smuggling. Or, I'll call her if you like. I'll have a chap pick up the package at her hotel. Herbert Booth. Where'd you tell me she stops?"

"The Bellamy."

"Ah, yes. Not a place I know. I'll jot it down. She may be annoyed for a moment, but with her love of mystery and intrigue she'll be amused and think it was like the Orient Express." He smiled down at Sydney and touched the tip of her nose affectionately with his forefinger.

She was almost convinced. "I admit I'm delighted that I don't have to ask her. But if customs makes her open the package? I know they seldom do, but it is a possibility."

"A rather slim one, I should think. Her receipt from the store saying it's an antique should satisfy them."

"Customs may be satisfied but Kim would be somewhat surprised I think."

"Have you a better plan?"

"No. The more I thought about asking her, the harder it was," she admitted. Then she laughed. "I suppose her immediate conclusion would be that I had played one of my jokes on her and switched packages."

"There may be some value in that diabolical streak you have after all." He glanced around at the sound of footsteps. "Ah, here are the others. Let's have you go along. You have a bit of a drive to Limerick."

 "I always stay here when I'm in Limerick," Sydney was saying as they were shown to their room. "I hate those new motel/hotel type places they've built near the airport. And it's only half an hour away. I thought we'd just share a room. We did so well together in Dublin." She felt a little guilty knowing it was chicanery, not camaraderie, that prompted her decision. She needed this proximity to switch the packages. But it would be such fun to laugh with Kim about the joke when it was all over. "Isn't it charming?"

"It's delightful." Kim pushed back the curtains and looked down from the long window. "Is that really the River Shannon?"

"It really is." Sydney stood behind her and looked over her shoulders across rooftops at the river, rather than straight down. "Like a painting, isn't it? Or a scene on an old stereopticon."

"Are those sea gulls over by the river?"

"Yes. We're very near the Atlantic, you know. Come on, let's change and take a walk beside the river. Then an early dinner and to bed. I hate a long flight when I'm tired, don't you?"

"You won't have to persuade me to get to bed early. I'm still a little hung. And I've walked more the last few days than I walk in a month at home."

"I'm taking a shower. Want me to steam anything for you?"

It was just like the old theatre days, wearing shower caps to protect hair-dos and turning the bathroom into a steam room.

"Yes, please. I'll wear this navy tomorrow, I think." She quickly put her dress on a hanger and handed it over.

After Sydney disappeared into the bathroom she set the room to order, stowing umbrellas and raincoats in the closet, putting purses in drawers as if they were staying a week. Scott, who never put anything away, always teased her about this habit of turning hotel rooms into temporary homes. After a few moments only the Meissen shepherdess was still lying on one of the beds. She started to put it in a drawer and then changed her mind. She never knew afterward why after all that time she suddenly *had* to open the package.

"I'm going to have one little peek at my shepherdess," she called. "Will you help me repack it?"

Sydney, startled, came out wrapped in a towel.

"Oh don't, luv, it's so safely packed and we're tired." Sydney's voice was muffled as she closed the door again. "Can't you wait one more day to admire it?"

"We've been over rough roads. Do you suppose she could be broken? I have to see right now."

Kim managed to slide the twine off the ends without having to cut it. The paper and packing came away easily. She lifted the wrapped figurine out carefully, laid it on the bed and pulled away the cotton.

"Sydney!" she screamed.

"Oh, no! Is it broken?" Sydney came running from the bathroom slithering into a green silk shirt.

On the bed lay a small bronze figure with a ridiculous half-moon shaped headdress.

"Jesus, where did *that* come from?"

"I don't know. It was in the package. My Meissen shepherdess package." Kim sank down on one of the beds on the verge of tears. "My shepherdess is lost. It's gone." Her mouth quivered.

"Dear heart, don't take on so. They must have made a mistake in the shipping room at Brown Thomas. Now, don't worry. We'll get it straightened out in the morning." Thank God it was too late to call now. She needed a little time to work this all out.

"Do you think the little people have taken my shepherdess?" She smiled weakly.

"*What* little people? What are you talking about?"

"The little green men who sit on toadstools?"

"Kim! You're falling apart."

"Well, do you think some other customer has my Meissen?"

"I'm sure of it—and you have their little idol—though who'd want it I'd never guess." Sydney picked it up and turned it over. It was a peculiar green color and very smooth to touch.

"Do you suppose it is old?"

Sydney shrugged. "How should I know?"

"We need Henry James to identify him."

"Him? I can't even tell what sex it is. Heavens, I don't think it's valuable or anything like that. It looks like one of those museum reproductions. Perhaps the original is something famous but I've never seen it."

"Do you think I'll get my shepherdess back?"

"Of course," Sydney assured her. "It's just like my weavers. Problems, problems. Little annoyances that drive us to distraction but they always work out." She slipped into sandals and tucked the silk shirt into straw-colored linen pants. "Are you ready for our walk? We'll get the little nasty to his proper owner and get your treasure back, never fear. You're with the right girl to handle this sort of thing."

As Kim searched for a sweater, Sydney looked at herself in the mirror and made a face. Why, oh why, do I always have to grab the ball and run? Too impulsive, that's what I am. When Kim was telling the maid about her Irish ancestors I should have told her about mine too, instead of playing sleight-of-hand artist. I think my story was ingenious enough for Ian. Wonder who this rich man in Connecticut is who'd want such a thing for his wife. Oh, well, she concluded, it will probably all turn out fine.

Dinner was not very good or very much fun.

Kim was tired and ready for bed but she knew she couldn't sleep.

Sydney would never admit that she hadn't slept well or that her conscience was troubling her. Thank goodness Kim had an early flight. She couldn't ring Brown Thomas before they left the room.

"You go check in," Sydney instructed as they entered the Shannon lounge for international flights. "I'll check on the shepherdess."

She dialed the operator and asked for the number for maritime weather. She smiled, cooed into the mouthpiece, turned around to see if Kim was able to see her, pointed to the phone, nodded, grimaced, kept on talking. The performance was of audition quality with many extravagant gestures and shrugs.

Kim, waiting for her ticket to be checked, watched anxiously as she inched toward the counter. She was astonished by the intensity of her feeling of loss but it was compounded by so many new feelings. She realized she was entirely disoriented. She also admitted to herself that the high life she had looked forward to so eagerly that morning in Florence had placed her way beyond her depth.

The drinking alone had put her at a disadvantage. She was like a child who had been allowed to stay up for a grownup party. Ian had made her heart skip beats and the night in the park with Henry, which seemed silly and childish now, had moved her then to giggles and tears. Even Walter Carrasco—was he really a gangster—had turned her head. For just a little while she had tried to be like Sydney, witty and airy and irresponsible. But she wasn't like that. She probably would not even have bought the shepherdess on a whim if it had not been for Sydney's influence. Now that she no longer had it she realized how important it was to her. Really, she didn't envy Sydney. She couldn't see that life as a permanent arrangement but she had luxuriated in the sheer frivolity of the whole week. Now everything was going by too fast and as she reached out to hold onto some of it, that too melted away. If she did not recover the shepherdess she was about ready to admit it had never existed.

She felt great relief when she saw Sydney smiling as she hurried across the big room.

"It's more complicated than I'd hoped. But the shepherdess is safe,"

Sydney hastened to assure her. "They sent it by air to a gift shop in Connecticut and only discovered the mistake when the shop called wondering what had happened to their horrid guy."

"Is he an antique too?"

"No. Just a reproduction."

"Where in Connecticut? How will I get it back?"

"They asked if you would take their package along with you as it is promised for delivery tomorrow. They will have a Mister...oh, what's his name. Wait. I wrote it down." She searched for a scrap of paper. "A Mister Booth will call for it. I told them you'd be at the Bellamy. It's a wonder I remembered the name."

"I always stay there because Dad first took me there as a little girl."

"I know, it seems unlikely for him too."

"He had a patient who lived right nearby on Park...."

"I know, and it was convenient and he got attached to the little bar and the bellmen all know him. Anyhow, you don't mind, do you? It really will not be much trouble and the situation is complicated enough already."

"If you're sure it isn't valuable. I hate to be responsible for other people's things. How much do you suppose it's worth?"

"Not much. Maybe forty or fifty pounds at most."

"And Mister Booth will bring my shepherdess."

"Right. He'll come to the hotel with it."

"Does he know how old it is? I hope he's careful."

"Luv, I expect he's careful. In a shop he must handle fragile things every day."

"Oh, Sydney, I'm a goose, but I fell in love with that statue. You see, my grandmother had one like it...."

"I know," Sydney interrupted.

"Not exactly like it. Hers was dressed in pink and I don't know if it was Meissen, but having this one makes me feel close to her and to myself when I was little, and even close to Ireland in a way. Do you see?"

"Yes, I do, really," Sydney relented. "I love Ireland because I have Irish ancestors too. When I come here I feel I am looking back at a part of myself. I even kissed the Blarney Stone once when I was here with Townie. He must have dared me to do it. You have to practically stand on your head and you know how I am about heights. I was probably terrified. But I was younger then and felt I had a lifetime to do foolish things."

"Thank you," Kim said fervently, "for working it out. You promised that you would but I kept thinking about it. I hardly slept last night."

"Poor dear. Come on, you still have time for the shop before you have to board. It's one of the best duty-free shops anywhere. Let me check your coat and umbrella and those things through to the plane so you don't have to carry them."

"This too?" Kim asked as Sydney reached for the package.

"Why not? It will be safe and you might leave it on a counter here. Don't let me utter that thought. After all we've been through already," and she tucked the package under her arm. "Wait until you see the shop."

Kim gave up the package with some misgiving. She would never have relinquished the Meissen.

"I'll get my ticket and turn in the car and be off."

"What is the man's name?" Kim asked nervously. "The one who's bringing my shepherdess?"

"Booth. Stop worrying, luv. Just remember, Booth like in telephone, or Edwin, if you prefer."

They hugged.

"I have to go to the coast soon so perhaps we can meet. Good-bye, dear heart. It's been marvelous. You're even better than I remembered."

"So are you—but the way you live! It would kill me."

Sydney laughed affectionately as she watched Kim vanish to be blissfully restored by bargains.

In twenty minutes Kim bought half an ounce of Joy, tried on a tweed suit she decided she could live without and when the boarding call came she was just unfolding a cutwork tablecloth.

"Plenty of time if you like this," the saleswoman said.

"I'm not sure I like it all that much, and having to leave makes up my mind." She had thought of taking some Irish Mist. Oh well. She paid for her purchase and moved toward the plane.

An enormously fat woman occupied the middle seat and on the aisle sat an equally fat man.

"I'm sorry," Kim smiled. "I believe I have the window seat."

Wouldn't they have been much more comfortable in aisle seats across from one another. They both obligingly, but with much difficulty, unwedged themselves and let her slide through.

As Sydney stood in line to get her ticket she felt momentarily a bit wicked for tricking Kim. She had said you can't be a little dishonest. Of course you can, dear heart, Sydney smiled to herself, especially if you don't know it. She dismissed the whole thing from her mind as she put the boarding pass in her pocket and moved to the car rental desk. There was a queue. Apparently a flight had just arrived, and eager Americans were signing up for their first taste of driving on what they considered the wrong side of the road.

A porter was walking past and she hailed him.

"It's the dark green Ford parked in the loading zone just by the door." She handed him the keys. "There is one bag, a raincoat and an umbrella on the back seat. I need to take something out of the bag. I'll be waiting in line."

She didn't dare chance Kim's shepherdess getting broken in her suitcase. She moved forward a pace. A radio behind the desk promised clear skies through tomorrow, and the Americans beamed.

"You'll be having fine weather for driving." The red-haired woman at the counter smiled as if she were happy for them and Sydney mused once again on the delightful Irish.

The clerk was handing back her credit card when the man returned with her things. She removed the shepherdess and sent him to check her bag. The announcer finished the weather and began unctuously reading the news. She was only half listening to a bulletin describing a small bronze antiquity, worth half a million pounds, a national treasure stolen from a private museum in Dublin. She stared at the radio in horror. Could it be the ghastly green figure that Kim was taking to New York?

"Jesus!" she gasped, nearly knocking down a middle-aged couple as she fled to the newsstand.

The ridiculous figure in Kim's package was on the front page. As she scanned the headlines, she saw through the great windows that the airplane had not left.

Sydney was so shaken she sat down on a bench. She tried to remember just what Ian had told her. Reproduction, indeed! Only off by a decade, eh? Perhaps two? The sheer brazenness of the deception took her breath away. She also pushed aside sneaking admiration for his daring, but fear for Kim prevailed. While she was pondering how she could get on the airplane and right things, a familiar figure appeared heading for the duty-free shop. Walter Carrasco was always turning up unexpectedly.

"Walter!" she called out. He could help somehow. But even near hysteria, she dared not tell him the truth.

"Sydney, darling." His handsome face was alight with pleasure. "What a great surprise, and what rotten luck that I am just leaving. Or are you on your way to New York, too?"

"No, luv, just back to London. But you're going to New York?"

A plan was forming in her facile mind but she could not rush too much. She glanced out the window again. How much more time did she have?

"I thought I was going to miss the damn plane. A gypsy caravan got in front of me and you know you can't get around horses on those narrow roads. Then I find the plane delayed and I was just going to buy something for Mamma and I see you. My lucky day."

Distracted, Sydney beamed at him, all the time scheming furiously.

"Wish I could buy you a drink or something but I'm afraid to get out of sight of that pretty girl in green by the door. She's going to call me when I have to get aboard."

"Too early for a drink, really. But you *can* do something for me." She lowered her voice and whispered conspiratorially, "I have a marvelous joke to play on Kim only I need a confederate and I didn't have one until you turned up."

"So, I'm the patsy," Walter groaned good-naturedly, remembering other jokes of hers.

"All you have to do is switch packages. Remember the little Meissen shepherdess she bought?"

"Yes. But I didn't get to see it."

"She'll show it to you when you give back the package at the Bellamy." Sydney was handing him the package as she talked.

"That's all I have to do?" He laughed. "Wait. You're going too fast. Where's Kim? Oh, on the airplane." He answered his own question, looking out toward the runway.

"You'll be sure to switch them so the joke will work?"

The airline girl was beckoning him.

"Okay. See you longer next time." He kissed her quickly and followed the young woman through the doorway, carrying the parcel.

The door shut almost as soon as Walter entered. It was shameful to arrange for him to take the stolen treasure into New York rather than Kim, but he was accustomed to handling difficult, dangerous situations just in case this turned out to be one. Sydney could hear the engines of the big jet as she turned back into the hollowness of the terminal. For the tenth time since she heard the bulletin she wondered if there were morning papers on the aircraft.

Her London flight was being called.

"Please bring me a Scotch and soda," she said as soon as they were airborne, "and some letter paper."

She pulled down the little tray and began to write.

Kim dearest,

I'm writing this on the way to London. I'll talk with you before you get it so it is a purely selfish letter. They say confession's good for the soul and at this moment mine is sorely troubled.

I believed Ian's story that it is a reproduction he needed to get to a client for a birthday gift. I knew I'd be in London long before you reach New York and I planned to call you before Mr. Booth arrived to pick up the package and explain that I have your shepherdess and it is safe.

I swear to God I didn't know it was stolen. When I learned in the airport that the damn thing is hot I nearly went into hysterics.

Just how could she make Kim believe that it had sounded innocent and simple when Ian mentioned it? Now she could trace the whole plot and see where she had been duped. But she had been so preoccupied with her curtain problems she hadn't paid much attention to Ian's story. It seemed plausible enough, that is, if you're a little dishonest yourself, she admitted in a moment of self-loathing.

"Would you like another drink?"

Had she already finished one?

She went on writing.

Then Walter came along and I saw a solution. When he agreed to switch packages he didn't know the real story either. While I'm confessing, I may as well admit that I couldn't resist the thrill of involving you in a little innocuous smuggling. What I hadn't counted on was that you'd insist on opening it. For a moment I panicked, but you know good old resourceful Sydney. How did you like the Brown Thomas phone call bit? Am I still a good actress? Or just a good crook? That didn't sound right, not quite the way she wanted. *You know me, ha, ha, ha.* She added.

She paused, thinking what to say next.

Please believe I've called myself all kinds of names and I will see that everything is straightened out.

Exciting anyhow, isn't it? Imagine that funny-looking thing being worth all that money! Sure fooled me.

Luv,

She addressed the envelope in her bold, confident hand and had it ready to post at Heathrow.

In seven hours, give or take, she could call Kim in New York. Those hours would pass slowly.

She shuddered. The moment they landed she would call Ian.

Women, even beautiful ones, are hardly worth the trouble, Walter sighed as he dropped into his seat in the first class section. This morning he thought he was going to miss his plane. He was driving the rented Jaguar like a demon all the way and then he got hung up behind that gypsy caravan. When he reached the airport there was just enough time to buy a present for Mamma. And then he ran into Sydney.

He adored her, but sometimes her pranks could get a man into difficulties. If this caper had anything illegal about it—and Sydney was not above a little smuggling he'd just bet—it wouldn't be too good for him right now. The job he had come over to do had been a headache from the moment he landed. The only pleasant time he looked back on was the afternoon he showed Naples in Ireland to Sydney and Kim. Maybe he'd retire to the real Naples someday. Start a little business there. He sighed again.

If The Boss was unhappy, and that was likely, Walter would be 'on vacation' for a while, not knowing what went wrong, how he had failed. He looked around at his fellow passengers. How nice to be just a happy tourist, or an ordinary business traveler. He felt very alone at that moment.

The package Sydney had given him was on the floor and he pushed it carefully under the seat ahead of him with his foot, wondering idly what was in it. He'd decide later how to make the exchange. Just then an attendant wheeled drinks down the aisle. She was very pretty and he was thirsty. He momentarily forgot about the parcels he had to juggle before they landed at Kennedy.

After a Bloody Mary he relaxed and it seemed a good idea to go back and invite Kim to join him. Also, he might see where she had stowed her package and consider the action. He looked through the curtains and saw her just getting up from a window seat on the right. It occurred to him this might be the moment for the swap. He went back for his parcel.

Two huge fatties were in the outside seats next to hers. He smiled at them.

"I was looking for Kim," he said fatuously, favoring them with a wink. "Is that that sweet girl's name?" The woman leaned over to her husband. "Isn't that a cute name for such a cute girl?"

"She'll be back in a minute," the man volunteered. "I think she's in the—you know." He jerked his thumb to the rear of the plane.

Walter saw the package just in front of Kim's empty seat. It was indeed identical to the one Sydney had given him.

"Excuse me." He bent down toward the fat woman. "Would you just hand me that package?" As the woman seemed to hesitate, he added, "I want to exchange it for one I just bought for her. A birthday surprise." The woman beamed and began to bend her great bulk forward to reach the birthday gift. At that instant the plane banked and Walter, off balance, landed across the laps of the two people. The woman lurched forward, pinning his head to the seat in front with her heavy bosom. In this prone position he was able to pick up Kim's parcel and substitute his own.

The man put out a beefy hand and extricated Walter from his wife's fleshly embrace and, as gracefully as possible, he apologized for disturbing them. The pair laughed uproariously. So good-natured, he thought as he turned to go.

"Don't mention what I've done," he cautioned, winking again, and they gleefully agreed to be accomplices.

He saw Kim walking toward him from the far end of the aisle. There was nothing to do but stuff the package under his jacket and let her think he was a slob who went around with packages bulging under his coat.

"Kim," he called.

"Walter!" *Her* surprise was genuine.

"I'm up here. Come have a drink with me." He took her by the arm and propelled her up the aisle. With the other arm he held the package in place. Every step of the way he was cursing Sydney for the predicament she had gotten him into.

There was no one sitting beside him and he gave Kim the window seat.

"Would you like a paper, sir?" The attendant was smiling down at them.

"Do you have a New York one?"

"No. Only London or Dublin."

"Either one, it doesn't matter." He put the folded paper on his lap and turned back to Kim.

She was telling him in great detail about a country house she visited yesterday with friends of Sydney's.

"And there was a cemetery on the grounds just for animals, mostly dogs. You could tell by the names that some were purebreds and some were just mutts. I felt so sad and loved that family who had thought so much of their pets." She smiled at him with eyes shiny from tears.

He was beginning to feel protective about this dear girl and hoped Sydney's joke was not too awful. Sometimes she could be quite ghoulish, he remembered.

Kim had noticed that Walter looked odd and seemed jumpy and now, as he turned to listen to her, his coat shifted away from him. Did gangsters really wear shoulder holsters? If he was wearing one on an airplane he must have a permit for a gun, so it was all right. She shivered and wondered again who his boss could be.

"Excuse me for a second," Walter said. "I'll find the hostess and see if you can have lunch with me." And get rid of this damn package, he added to himself.

"Oh, that would be fun. Thank you."

I really do like him, Kim thought. No need to dwell on his profession. She was safe enough with him here on the plane. Maybe it was just one of Sydney's jokes after all. He was probably an ordinary businessman with international connections. The idea reassured her and she reached for the Dublin paper.

The front page put Walter right out of her head. She gasped.

"Are you all right?" asked a man sitting across the aisle.

"Yes," she smiled wanly. "I'm a terrible sissy about flying. Every time we dip or turn I panic." There had been no perceptible movement.

It was a lie. She was beginning to be afraid of several things but flying was not one of them.

"It's a nice bright day," the man tried to be reassuring. "Should be a smooth flight all the way." He returned to his magazine.

Kim looked at the paper, hoping it was all a bad dream. NATIONAL TREASURE MISSING, the headline screamed. There was the picture and an article describing the little green figure. It was stolen and valued at half a million pounds. She tried to translate into dollars but gave up.

She was far too upset to sit here chatting with Walter over lunch. As she got up to leave, Walter reappeared.

"It's all set."

"I'm sorry, Walter. I feel ill. Lightheaded, as if I might faint."

She did look pale. "Sit down," he urged. "I'll get a wet towel. Put your head between your knees, they say."

"Really thanks, I'd like to go back to my own seat."

He kept insisting.

"No, really, thanks." She almost bolted down the aisle to one of the washrooms. She thought she was going to be sick but when she washed her face with cold water, she was able to stagger back to her seat.

The fat couple struggled to their feet, looking at her curiously. The package was safe anyhow, still under the seat ahead. She would have to think of facing customs. Should she walk up to the first person in uniform and say, "I have the national treasure that's missing"? No doubt it was in the New York papers by now and they would understand. Would they *believe* her, though? She hardly looked like a member of an international smuggling ring. But they'd believe her when she opened the box. No. That would be stupid. She couldn't explain how she happened to have the thing. It would sound too silly.

An ugly thought kept creeping forward. Had Sydney known? Had she deliberately done this to her? *Could* it have been a mistake at the store? Or Walter? Why hadn't she thought of him at once? He was a gangster. But was that a reason to be suspicious? He might not be involved at all. But he acted so odd. And she was sure he had a gun under his coat.

Perhaps there will be a long delay over Kennedy. Or maybe we'll crash, she thought wildly, and I'll never have to face it.

Walter kept coming back to see how she was feeling and she was barely polite. She didn't want lunch; she didn't want a drink. Finally she lay back with her eyes closed.

Hell, what can I do if she is going to act like that. Let those fat people worry about her. They seemed to be enjoying it. Every time he came back they gave him a knowing look. After all the package nonsense, they were probably imagining that there had been a lovers' quarrel. He sighed and picked up his copy of the Dublin paper.

"Well, we're lucky today, folks," the homespun voice of the captain was broadcasting. "We're going right in without delay."

The fat man smiled at Kim. "No delay. That's unusual."

"Yes," she murmured.

"You feelin' better, hon?" the woman asked.

Kim nodded. She was trapped behind their bulk as they inched along the aisle, but as soon as they were off the plane she managed to lose them.

There were long lines in front of each customs officer. She stood for a moment trying to find one who looked jolly and friendly, but that one didn't appear to exist. She joined the nearest line. In her hand she clutched the slip Brown Thomas had given her. It read, "Figurine, circa 1820." That was all. She hoped if she was asked to open the package there would be only a glance and no questions.

Kim put her hand luggage on the counter in front of the man. He inquired about liquor and she began to tell him she had intended to bring a bottle of Irish Mist but at the last minute decided against it.

He couldn't have cared less.

"Any gifts you're carrying?"

She showed the perfume stuffed in her oversize purse.

"What's in this package?"

"An antique figurine I bought in Dublin." Her voice may have sounded all right to him, but it was false in her own ears. She handed him the damp, wrinkled slip of paper and noticed that her fingers trembled. He glanced at the receipt from the store and returned it, asking where she'd been and how long.

"Italy, England, Ireland, for twenty-one days," she answered, as she fumbled with the lock.

He poked into the contents with an experienced hand and waved her on.

She had to get to a telephone and call London. Sydney would be home by now.

Kennedy was the usual madhouse; thousands of frantic hurrying people, phones all in use. No one was paying any attention to anyone else. At last there was a phone.

Circuits to London busy.

She thought of calling Scott and realized that was useless.

Her father's line was busy.

As she hesitated, looking around, a porter grabbed her suitcase and somehow managed to get the package too. Over his shoulder he said, "I'll meet you by the taxi stand," and was gone. She hadn't signaled him but she probably was looking uncertain as if she wanted a porter. She tried to run after him but he had already melted into the crowds. As she turned around she noticed a strange-looking man who seemed to be watching her with sinister amusement.

You're imagining things," she told herself. What was strange about the man? He was wearing a grey summer suit, a shocking pink shirt and a pink and grey tie—garish enough, but men's clothes were so colorful these days.

He was extremely slim and yet he didn't look ill or particularly fragile.

Then why had she noticed him at all?

Because just before she looked up she had the definite feeling that someone was watching her and there he was.

The porter was waiting with her bag. She retrieved the package, and as she climbed into a cab she noticed that the man in the grey suit had moved out to the sidewalk.

Walter observed that they were checking hand luggage carefully. He had long ago formed the habit of noticing this kind of detail. Today he was carrying nothing to worry about, but it would be wise to take a look at Kim's shepherdess so he could describe it if they asked questions.

The washroom was empty. The string was tough and he used his knife on it. Several layers of packing pulled away.

"Jesus, Mary and Joseph!"

It was not a piece of Meissen at all. It wasn't even ceramic. It was the thing he'd been reading about on the plane. Stolen and worth half a million pounds. There was no doubt. The picture in the Irish paper was clear and he had read the story with a good deal of professional interest.

He'd been framed by a damn broad. Kim seemed so pretty and innocent, crying over a graveyard full of dogs. He wouldn't have thought it. The Boss always did say they were the ones to look out for. But it was Sydney who gave him the package. Were they in it together or had Kim been framed too? How could Sydney have gotten mixed up in a thing like this? It must have something to do with her business. Was it possible she didn't know what she was doing? Possible, but hardly likely. She was shrewd and clever but he never thought of her as dishonest. She went in for jokes but this was no joke.

She had accused him of playing a bad joke on her when she got into such a hassle over taking a gun for him from Huatulco to Oaxaca. He had no idea security would be so tight on that little hop. In spite of himself he chuckled now thinking how ridiculous she looked standing there in the police station with a diamond on one hand and an emerald on the other, and handcuffs so loose they almost slipped over her slim wrists. He'd felt like a shit-ass and told her so when he got it straightened out. They had laughed over a drink and she said she'd get even.

She was even now, and more.

He looked at the object in his hand. It could pass for one of those plaster copies you saw in Brentano's window at Christmas.

He couldn't stay here. The contents of the package he put into his raincoat pocket. He stuffed the paper, packing and string in the trash, pulled half a dozen paper towels from the dispenser and dropped them on top.

He hadn't had such a hell of a good trip as it was and if The Boss ever learned about this complication he'd have had it.

"Nothing," he said when the officer questioned him about what he was carrying. Long ago he learned that it never paid to talk to customs inspectors but today he was unusually curt. And he had one who wanted to strike up a conversation.

"No liquor?" His glance said Walter looked like the kind of guy who would bring in a bottle. "Everybody on these flights from Ireland brings something. The women some fancy thing—men it's hard to tell. Martini drinkers bring gin and there's not much saving on that. No imagination, the men. On the other hand, women bring stuff they can't drink. Some kind of sweet liqueur."

"I almost missed the plane," Walter explained. "Not enough time." He was wiping his forehead. I wish to hell I had missed the plane, he thought. I wish those Gypsies had slowed me down a whole lot more.

"Okay. Next time bring a bottle," the man advised and waved him on.

There was no sign of Kim, though he saw the fat couple and avoided them. Now that he was through customs what should he do? Stuff it in the nearest trash can? He had learned early on from The Boss that this is the way amateurs get caught. Obviously go to the hotel and give it to Kim. He began to sort out the situation in his mind. Kim carried it onto the plane so she knew about it. Or did she? Sydney conned him with the wild joke story, so she knew. He nodded. Yes, Sydney knew any way you figured it. She couldn't have pulled it off alone so somebody else knew. Who? One thing was sure, he had done the hard part. He was the fall guy who carried it off the plane. Into the United States. He whistled at the enormity of his entanglement as he walked through the electric door to the cab stand.

Kim hadn't checked in when he reached the Bellamy. Walter stood in the lobby wondering if he should have a drink or call The Boss or go away and come back later.

Finally he walked out of the hotel still trying to make sense of the whole thing. He'd been duped but maybe he could make something out of it. Instinct told him he shouldn't try. He had been on a specific assignment and that hadn't worked. The Boss wouldn't like him to take on something on his own. It was tempting as hell, though. If the thing was valued at half a million pounds you could bet it was being sold for at least twice that. Getting it into New York ought to bring a good price.

A crowd had gathered around the corner in front of a television store. He glanced between heads to see what was attracting attention. Red SALE signs pointed to half a dozen color sets all tuned to the same channel. The screens were filled with a familiar green figure.

"Jesus, Mary and Joseph," he muttered, clapping his hand to his coat pocket. He began to shove his way through the crowd to get inside.

A strident-voiced woman was arguing with a salesman and he had to bend over to hear the announcer's voice. He got only the tag end but it said there was a report that the figure might have been taken to New York. It sure as hell had.

His mind was made up. No deals. Get rid of the damn thing. But he didn't. What really bothered him, he admitted to himself, was Sydney. That lovely creature. How did she fit this puzzle? He walked into his mother's living room with the stolen object still in his pocket.

Mamma placed a bottle of Frascati on the table along with two glasses. It was a ritual when he returned from a trip. Interesting, he thought, we always drink Frascati rather than something from near Naples. Maybe he should retire to Frascati. Where the hell was it? Close to Rome? The Boss liked Frascati and Mamma thought what The Boss liked was good for them too.

She never asked him how things went; he just told her. No specifics ever. But he could talk about what he pleased and what troubled him. It was difficult today. Nothing had gone well and later he would have to face The Boss. He had an added weight on his mind from the weight in his pocket. He took several sips of the cool wine before he said anything.

"Mamma, what if someone you like a lot, might even love, appeared to have tricked you? In a big, important, dangerous way? What would you do?"

"You're not sure? Maybe?"

He thought a long time before he answered. Finally he shook his head. "Not sure."

"I'd make sure before I did anything."

The bottle was empty when he kissed his mother goodbye.

He had done all the talking as usual. She had just listened. Talking had convinced him of two things. Sydney just could not be guilty as he had imagined earlier. He knew her too well to believe she could do a thing like that. And Kim was in more danger than he had imagined earlier.

He was clear in his resolve now. Kim would be safer without the object so he'd put it in a safe place. He would make his report to The Boss and then go to her hotel. He would find out what was going on if he had to kick the door down to get in.

If Ian was there he was not answering. Sydney let it ring. He'd never have a machine answer for him. Too ordinary. She shook her head. She didn't have a machine, either. But the hotel had a switchboard. He just might not wish to speak to her—or to anyone. Finally she returned the receiver.

For the umpteenth time she looked at her watch. It would still be hours before she could reach Kim in New York.

"Come in," Sydney called when there was a knock. She had, many of her friends thought, a bad habit of not securing locks.

Ian opened the door and came in, for him tentatively.

"I've been calling you."

"I thought you might have been. May I explain?"

"Try."

"I was transporting the object for a rich client as I told you. What I didn't tell you was that he was paying a million pounds. I didn't know it was stolen."

"Somehow I don't believe you."

"Somehow I thought you wouldn't, darling."

"You stole that object and you let me set Kim up."

"I removed the object from the museum as you are surmising. Had it removed, actually. Everything would have been all right but Danny O'Rahilly tricked me."

"Who's Danny O'Rahilly?"

"Calcularius."

"The magician?"

"He's done several jobs for me over the years and performed well. This important one he botched. He killed the guard. He didn't tell me the plaster replacement was broken. It's all his fault."

"Oh, Jesus! And you killed Danny O'Rahilly."

He moved toward her casually, his coat open, his hands in his pockets. It shouldn't have been threatening, but it was. Sydney took a step back and too late realized she was standing in the open doorway, the balcony behind her. She panicked, remembering a conversation she and Townie had once about a scene in a play in which she was attacked and knew she would be killed.

"I would scream," she had told him. "And scream and SCREAM!"

That was the way she played the scene. Audiences loved it. So did the critics, she remembered. It was all true, your life flashed past in a matter of seconds when you were about to die.

Ian had removed a small gun from his pocket and was advancing slowly. She didn't scream.

"Shoot me, please," she murmured. It was a desperate plea.

Yes, the balcony was behind her and she had never stepped out on it in all the years since she first came here as a child.

He was still moving slowly toward her, a small smile playing around his lips.

"This is a shame," he said softly. "I'm truly fond of you."

She stepped back yet another foot.

"Please shoot me."

"Far too messy. And the five-floor fall is much more accidental in point of fact." He returned the gun to his pocket. He knew by now that she was immobilized like a frightened mouse being taunted by a lazy cat that could wait as long as it wished before springing.

He took an almost idle step forward.

Sydney did not step back.

They were face to face, only inches apart.

"I don't expect this is going to be easy. For either of us."

She thought she was speaking but there was no sound. Her head was spinning. Her knees gave way. She didn't fall. She crumpled.

She was tall but she was slim. Ian lifted her without effort and rolled her gently over the low railing.

He didn't have to look. He had checked the awning as he passed on his way to the back stairs. A clean drop to the concrete. It was much easier than he had anticipated. For both of them.

"So sorry, old dear."

No one had seen him enter.

No one saw him leave.

He cut through the service drive to White Horse and joined the foot traffic moving away from Piccadilly.

"The Bellamy," Kim said as she settled her things on the seat of the taxi.

A puzzled narrow dark face peered over the seat separating them. She gave him the address. No indication that he understood.

"Wait." She wrote the address on a slip of paper.

He nodded and shot out into traffic.

After that first jump he was patient and did fairly well in airport traffic.

Then they moved into the multi-laned real thing.

He changed lanes erratically, speeding past other fast-moving vehicles. He tailgated.

"Be careful!" Kim leaned forward and almost slid onto the floor as he braked suddenly.

She shut her eyes but that was too scary.

She tried looking out the side window but the blurred landscape changed so fast it made her dizzy.

She should pray. To whom? For what? She tried to remember words of a childhood prayer but the only one she could recall was the bedtime one and the line, "If I should die before I wake...."

When she glanced ahead they were only inches from a van.

PLEASE DRIVE CAREFULLY

Huge letters on the back of the vehicle so close they appeared to be on the taxi windshield.

"Watch out!" Kim screamed.

He pushed the brake pedal almost through the floor and they barely tapped the rear of the van.

Kim's lurch stopped as the edge of the seat caught her just under the right eye. A muffled "Uhh" was her only sound.

"Are you crazy?" Kim straightened up in time to see the driver jump out of the taxi, zigzag through traffic and disappear.

"What the fuck you think you're doing?" The delivery van driver leaned through the open door into the front seat and only then realized there was no one there.

"Where the hell is he?" the man shouted at Kim.

"How the fuck should I know," she shouted back. Fuck was a word her mother never allowed. She didn't like it either, but it gave great satisfaction to use it now. She giggled.

"What's so goddamn funny? That bastard hit my van and now he's gone."

Her cheekbone was throbbing and her eye kept tearing. She looked around. The package was safe on the seat beside her. After all that had happened, this was unbelievable. She kept laughing. He'd never understand.

Traffic was snarled around them. Honking horns and loud oaths were deafening. The sirens were coming closer. She looked to see where they were. Somewhere in Queens, she'd guess.

The man from the delivery truck was somewhat calmer as he tried to explain what had happened. The police turned to her.

"Who was the driver? Can you describe him?"

"He was slight and dark. He had a thin face." She recalled him looking at her over the seat as she tried to explain how to get to the hotel.

"Puerto Rican—Mexican—Middle Eastern—what do you mean when you say dark?"

It was a racist question and there was no way to speculate except with a racist answer.

"I don't know."

"We're going to have to ask you to come to the station and answer some questions."

"I don't know anything. I just landed at Kennedy after a long flight. I'm trying to get to my hotel. This ridiculous thing happened. My head hurts. I don't know anything."

"Sorry."

Before she could protest further, a man in blue was driving the taxi to a police station.

At least he was a better driver.

The same questions. The same answers.

She doubted if she could identify the cab driver if she saw him.

She had no idea why he ran.

No, he wasn't a very good driver.

No, he didn't seem to understand English very well.

No, she couldn't identify his ethnic background.

They were nice enough.

Sergeant Gwendolyn Harris was concerned about her eye. She brought an ice pack. "You're going to have a good shiner."

"Do they call you Gwen?" Kim asked, looking at her name tag.

"No, they call me Gwendolyn."

And with respect, Kim thought as she looked at the almost six-foot blonde with a round, ruddy face.

The rookie who was assigned to drive her to the hotel looked about seventeen. He thought she might have a cracked cheekbone. Should see a doctor.

She felt less apprehensive now that she was inside the Bellamy. They were too discreet as she checked in to comment on her disheveled appearance or the bruise marks showing below the sunglasses she didn't need at this hour. And they were not fatuous enough to ask if she had a good flight.

The hotel hadn't changed much since her last visit. Hadn't changed much in fact since Dad brought her here when she was five or six. The lobby had the same deep wing chairs. The little bar looked cool and inviting. While she waited for a bellman she walked over and looked at the menu posted beside the dining room door. She certainly didn't look like going in for dinner but she was starving. When she was settled she'd call room service.

As Howard put her bag in the elevator she told him how delighted she was that he was still here and gave him greetings from her father.

He turned to her with pleasure. "Doctor Brennan was here last week. Nice man. We're always glad to see him."

As soon as the door closed, Kim went into the bathroom to survey the damage. Her right eye was swollen almost shut and there was an ugly black streak along her cheekbone. It was painful, but a shiner was the least of her worries at the moment.

She moved to the bed, slipped off her shoes and sat down. She picked up the telephone, tucking her feet under as if settling in for a chat. She was forcing herself to be calm as she began to place the long distance call.

"Operator, please get me London. It's an emergency," she added, giving the woman the Devon's number. It was a terrible hour to be calling but she *had* to speak to Sydney.

The package was lying on the bed beside her just as it had been in Limerick yesterday. Was it only yesterday? It seemed ages ago. It was too incredible. What would Sydney's explanation be? She looked through her purse until she found her nail scissors to snip the twine. There was a wait and the operator was asking for her name and room number. The wire clicked fast, and faint voices broke over one another as the call went through. With each click Kim's heart pounded.

"I'm sorry, Miss Reardon is not in," the Devon operator was saying in her efficient hotel voice. "She...." A hesitation.

"Tell her it's terribly important," Kim said. "This is Kimberleigh Brennan. I was in London with Miss Reardon last week. I *must* talk with her. The operator will remember me."

"There's been a frightful accident," the Devon operator blurted out, her switchboard manner shattered. "Miss Reardon fell from her balcony."

She was either unable to go on, thought better of it, or was shushed. There were other voices and the connection was broken.

"Fell from the balcony," Kim sobbed. "She couldn't have! It's not possible. She never went near the balcony."

"Would you care to re-place the call?"

"No," Kim said dully.

Her hand was shaking so violently she could hardly put the receiver back in the cradle. All the time she was talking she must have been removing the packing from the figure on the bed. Now, for the first time, she glanced at it.

"Dear God," she cried aloud. "What's happening?"

Sydney is dead. It had to be murder. *Had* to be. She was too terrified of heights to go near the balcony. She *couldn't* have fallen. She had to have been pushed.

Yesterday she had discovered she had the wrong statue and this morning she found it had been stolen and was valued at half a million pounds. Now she had the Meissen shepherdess again. Maybe the little people had taken it. Kim began to laugh and cry at the same time.

What should she do?

Call her father again.

Don't let it be busy now, she prayed as she dialed his private number. It was ringing.

"Hello," the deep familiar voice said.

"Dad. It's Kim. I'm so frightened."

The line went dead.

She was trapped. They knew she had the stolen object. Only she didn't have it. Who are "they"? She didn't know. But she did know she was not intended to leave this room alive. A hotel room was impersonal and desolate if you were alone, even when you were not in trouble. At this moment it was terrifying. If Sydney could be killed in her own apartment at the Devon, then why couldn't Kim Brennan be done away with in a hotel in New York?

In characteristic style, she thought of herself as being in a play. Yes, it was very like *Desperate Hours* or *Kind Lady* or *Blind Alley*, those old melodramas, beloved of summer stock companies, where a woman is victimized by a criminal, and with help almost within calling distance, she isn't able to protect herself and waits despairingly for the end.

The telephone rang.

She grabbed it eagerly.

"Hello."

She could hear someone breathing.

"Hello, who is it?" There was no answer. "What do you want?" Her voice was high and squeaky.

"You know what I want," a voice said. Did he have a foreign accent or did she imagine it?

"Who are you? Are you the man who's been following me?" She was almost screaming now.

"No need to get excited. Tell me where I can pick up the package and you are in no danger."

"No danger," she repeated hollowly. "Are you Mister Booth?"

"Booth? Never heard of him. The package or...."

Before he could finish the threat she slammed down the receiver and began to rock back and forth on the bed, sobbing.

"Dear God, what am I going to do? Who will help me?"

Wait a minute. She had just been talking on the telephone. It was not dead. She could call the police. She reached for the phone and then hesitated as she realized how the conversation would go.

"Why didn't you report this as soon as you landed in New York, Miss Brennan?"

"I was in an accident in a taxi and I hit my head and the driver ran and I was taken to a police station."

"To a police station? And you said nothing about the stolen object?"

"I wanted to talk to my cousin in London first and find out what happened."

"Did you talk to your cousin?"

"No."

"Why not?"

"She's dead."

"Dead?"

"Murdered."

"And you still made no report to the police?"

"You see, I don't have the object now. I wanted to talk to my father and ask him what to do."

"Come now, Miss Brennan, would you have us believe...."

There was a rapid knocking at the door.

"Kim, Ian Hardwicke here."

"Ian, you, here?" She rushed to open the door.

The glorious Ian Hardwicke, splendid in a dark silk suit, a blue and white striped shirt and a black tie, let her rush into his embrace. He kept one arm around her shoulders while he pushed the door closed with the other and hooked the chain. Then he led her gently to a chair.

"Kimberleigh Brennan. Her room number please," Walter Carrasco said into a house phone.

"I'm sorry, we can't give out that information."

"Thanks." He put down the telephone and turned away. There was always a way to get a room number. Easily. Without wasting much time or money. Walter watched two or three bellmen come and go before he approached one.

"I need the room number for Kimberleigh Brennan." He held a twenty dollar bill in his hand.

"I'm sorry, sir. We're not allowed to give that out."

They all read from the same script.

"May I deliver a message?"

Walter smiled conspiratorially. "No. I have a surprise for her and I want to deliver it myself." He added another bill.

At sixty dollars they reached an understanding.

"Let me see if I may be able to help you."

From habit Walter looked both ways when he stepped off the elevator. He walked the corridor before he approached her door.

"Kim, it's Walter." He rapped lightly. "Let me in. The package is safe but you're in danger."

Ian whipped a gun from his pocket and held the barrel tight against Kim's temple. The index finger of his other hand was pressed against her lips.

It seemed an eternity but it couldn't have been more than a few seconds before the door opened until the chain caught it.

Walter never considered himself the physical type but he was frustrated and worried about Kim. He jammed his foot against the door and with one blow snapped the chain.

Ian swung the gun away from Kim. The eerie sound of the silenced shot was exaggerated in the quiet room.

Walter wasn't knocked off his feet like in television movies. Kim watched in horror as he looked startled for an instant and then crumpled backward, stretched on the floor with his head propped awkwardly against the leg of a chair. A stain spread slowly in the crotch of his pale summer suit.

Ian pushed the door shut, careful to keep the gun pointed.

"I think I'm going to be sick."

She turned toward the bathroom.

"Don't move."

She knew he had murdered Sydney. She had just watched him shoot Walter. Next he would kill her.

She didn't move as she threw up all over his expensive suit.

You had to admire him. He took a deep breath and wiped himself off with a paisley silk square from Liberty.

His face was only inches from hers. "Where is the package?"

"I don't know. I swear."

"That man said it is safe. Who is he? Was he?" he revised.

"Walter. Walter Carrasco. Sydney's friend. You didn't have to kill him."

"Didn't have to kill him? When he kicked down the door?"

"You're crazy. And now you're going to kill me." It sounded so matter-of-fact. She must be in shock to not try to run. He was going to shoot her anyhow in his own good time.

As if he read her thoughts he said, "Not quite yet, my dear. First, I'll have the package."

"I told you I don't have it. I thought I had it but when I opened the box it was my Meissen shepherdess."

"Then where is it?"

"I don't know."

He slapped her hard with the back of his hand. The heavy gold signet ring which must be the family crest he was so proud of split her lip and she cried out as she huddled out of reach.

Neither heard any sound in the hall and they both turned sharply when the door opened.

"Henry! What the hell are you doing here?"

"Following in your footsteps, as usual, Hardwicke."

Ian had laid the gun on the bed when Kim slipped to the floor. He started to reach for it.

"If you touch that nasty little piece I'll break your arm." Henry's voice was unusually raw. "Sit down. There are a few things to talk over." He helped Kim to her feet and handed her a handkerchief. "Your mouth is bleeding. Wipe it," He said gently. "You look bloody awful. Don't be afraid. It's all right now."

She sat down. Confused, but no longer terrified.

"I tried to make myself believe that nonsense about O'Rahilly and the political business, but there were too many loose wires. When I saw in the paper that he had been identified as the man found dead in an alley not far from the Liffey, the whole thing became clear."

"The man murdered in Dublin," Kim said. "He was the man who begged us for help. And you killed him?" She was overwhelmed by the enormity of his evil. "How could you?"

"I had to kill him. He was going to drag me in. And you too." He looked at Henry. "Danny tricked me. He didn't tell me that the plaster model was broken. He was not honest with me. That's what caused all the trouble."

"So, Danny wasn't honest? A thief wasn't playing the straight bat, eh? The little crook dared to lie to a member of the ascendancy, did he? You disgust me."

"What did that man have to do with you?" Kim finally found her voice and looked at Ian.

"He...worked for me."

"Worked for him," Henry said contemptuously. "He was a second-story man, you know, a cat burglar, they say in the trade. Before he became better known as a magician."

"Magician?" Kim was puzzled.

"Calcularius. He was a thief on the side. Trying to get papers so he could go to the United States. He was to steal the treasure and replace it with a fake."

"He dropped it!" Ian burst out indignantly.

"Otherwise that theft might have gone undetected for a long while," Henry explained. "I could have gone on trying to delude myself indefinitely."

"If O'Rahilly had just been honest with me, none of this would have happened," Ian repeated.

"We were all dishonest," Henry said flatly. "Ian, Danny, I was too, even Sydney a little."

"Did she...?" Kim was unable to voice it. She tried again. "Was she...?"

"A part of this sordid scheme?" Henry finished for her. "No, she believed the tale Ian told her. He said it was a birthday gift. Had to be in New York for delivery on Tuesday. Ian came up with this identical package for you to carry and Sydney was to bring your shepherdess when she came next week. You know Sydney and jokes. She probably thought this one was fun. And, she was afraid you'd think it was smuggling so she went along with switching the packages. I suppose she was a *little* dishonest."

"You can't be a *little* dishonest."

Henry smiled wistfully at her. "It's so simple for you. I can remember when it was that way for me. A long time ago. Before I became involved with this thief—this killer." He looked at Ian and shook his head.

All three were lost in thought for a long moment.

"But now I don't have the stolen figure. I have my shepherdess. And Walter said the piece was safe. How did he know?"

"Society is the thief," Ian said, paying no attention to Kim. "It stole my birthright. Younger sons never have a choice." He was very pale and his hands jerked as he clenched and unclenched them. "This was going to be the last time for me. I could have retired to a house in the country to live like my brother. To live better than Andrew," he mused. "You see there was no choice."

Henry sneered at Ian. "We all had choices. I finally had to face up to myself. I got on an airplane for London. I knew Sydney would put it all together when she saw the paper and you'd feel you had to kill her too. I was a little late."

He turned to Kim. "Ian doesn't know it, but Sydney is alive."

Ian started.

"Alive!" Kim cried. "But the operator said...Ian said...."

"She's in hospital. Two broken legs but she's going to live. Ian was certain she would die when she fell but that big awning over the terrace saved her."

"The awning was not out. I checked as I went in." Ian sounded amazed.

"Saved by the changeable London weather. It had only just been put out when you pushed her."

Ian lunged for the gun but Henry kicked it aside before he reached the bed. He was on top of him, holding him down with a knee on his chest. With both hands he lifted Ian's head and slammed it down on the carpet. He kept pounding his head over and over again, even after Ian was completely limp.

"Stop! Stop! Stop! You're going to kill him."

Henry James did not hear her.

Kim tried to drag him away but he shoved her aside.

"Freeze!" a big voice said.

Henry let Ian's head drop. He turned around slowly—very slowly— and looked up at the biggest Black man he had ever seen.

"Florian!" Kim ran sobbing into the giant's arms.

He signaled for the two uniformed officers behind him to wait in the hall. He looked down at her "What happened to you?" Without waiting for an answer, he reached for his card and badge, keeping a comforting arm around Kim.

"This procedure seem a little unusual?" He motioned for Henry to stand. "Florian Gibson, NYPD."

"He's a good friend of my father's," Kim explained.

Henry nodded, totally puzzled.

"What she really means is her dad is a good friend of mine. Saved my life once. Who are you?"

"Henry James."

"He's wonderful. He was trying to help me."

"Help you with what? I find a body over there." He looked at Henry. "I find you beating the shit out of somebody." He turned to Kim. "Tad said when you called you were scared to death. What's going on?"

"It's a long story," Kim said.

"Might we sit?" Henry was suddenly unbelievably tired.

"How did you find me? How did you know where I was?"

"Tad called me. Said he was talking to you when the phone went dead. There was one bitch of a storm there. He said if you were in New York you'd be here. You can bet I moved my ass to get over here.

"I've owed him one all these years," he explained to Henry. "Since the Sixties.

"They needed somebody to go to Mexico—way down almost to the bottom border—and bring back this bastard who had been moving drugs for years. With the help of every agency on both sides of the border they finally locked him up. I was a rookie and I said I'd go get him. Thought it would help my career.

"You know what a *papialbillo ahumado* is?"

Henry didn't know.

"It means smoked weasel, but when you say it with the right emphasis it comes out something like dumb nigger.

"I hadn't stepped off that little ten-seat plane before everybody in town knew why I was there.

"I checked into a fleabag of a hotel. Even that was a hassle. I started to walk across the street to the police station where they were holding this guy.

"WHAM-O!

"Luckily Tad Brennan drug me out of the alley before the rats chewed me up completely.

"After a day or two I opened my eyes and saw this beautiful white guy leaning over me holding a damp cloth to my head. He was on his honey-moon—down looking at some obscure ruins.

"While I was out of it, the jerk in jail disappeared. That trip didn't do a whole hell of a lot for my career. Thanks to the Brennans I lived through it, though. Didn't do a hell of a lot for their honeymoon, either. I ended up in their bed and they slept on the floor and took turns watching after me. I won't repeat what I told them." He grinned at Kim. "Your mother says she still blushes when she thinks about it. Ask her.

"Your dad never called in the marker until tonight. I'm glad I was there."

"So am I," Kim said with fervor.

Ian stirred.

Gibson nodded his head and one of the officers moved in from the hall. Ian was about to regain consciousness and find himself handcuffed.

Kim started to explain. "Ian killed Walter. He tried to kill Sydney. He killed Calcularius, too. He would have killed me but for Henry. He stole the little green man in Ireland."

Henry leaned back in his chair and looked at Florian Gibson with interest and something akin to sympathy. There was no way he was going to follow Kim's narrative.

"What little green man?"

"The one in the news valued at half a million pounds. I had it but now I don't."

Gibson had already realized it was going to take a long time and a lot of effort to make any sense of all this. He put up both hands. "We're going to have to go to the station to sort this out. You've lost me. We'll call Tad from there. Sorry, but you must come with me."

Henry put his arm around Kim's shoulders and they followed the big man to the elevator. He was in plenty of trouble but he could not remember a time in his life when he'd been happier.

Kim was on her way to a police station for the second time in just a few hours. But now she wasn't afraid. Henry was beside her and Florian Gibson was leading the way.

 Kim's conversation with her father was tearful and lengthy. "Here, take this." Florian Gibson lifted the telephone receiver from her hand and gave her a cup of coffee. "Sit down. I need to ask you some questions."

She looked across the room at Henry and he reassured her with a nod.

"The little green man. The stolen treasure worth half a million or so? You thought Sydney had been murdered? That body in the ice cream suit on the floor in your room sure as hell had been. How do we sort this all out? Where do we start?"

"I bought a Meissen shepherdess in Dublin. At Brown Thomas. It was an antique with no insurance so I was carrying it with me. For some reason I was worried about it and insisted upon opening the package in Limerick. Instead of my shepherdess, I had a strange little green man." She shrugged. "I guess it was a man. Anyhow, Sydney said it was probably a mistake at the store and we'd get it straightened out in the morning. I couldn't sleep thinking about my shepherdess. I know it's silly but it was so important because my grandmother had one like it and...."

Florian lifted his hand. "Okay. I understand. Back to the little green man."

"Well, Sydney called from Shannon and got the store and they said it was a mistake. They would send my shepherdess if I would just take the little figure and someone would come to the hotel in New York and exchange packages."

"Did anyone come to the hotel to make the exchange?"

"No, but you see Walter wanted me to have a drink with him on the plane and then I saw the newspaper and I knew the little man was priceless and stolen and I panicked. And on the way into town I had this crazy taxi driver and I was in an accident and I had to go to a police station and I had a black eye and when I reached the hotel it was late and I was a mess and I went upstairs and tried to call Sydney and learned about her accident and I thought she was dead and all the time I was on the telephone I must have been untying the package and when I opened it I had my shepherdess."

"Who's Walter?"

"May I?" Henry said, standing and moving over toward Kim and Florian Gibson. "I think I can shed some light on all this. If you will let me begin at the beginning."

"This is the most fucked-up story I ever heard. Be my guest if you can straighten out anything."

"When I finish you'll have to arrest me. Unfortunately I have been involved in the whole sordid affair."

"You have?" Kim began to cry. "I can't believe it. I don't want to believe it."

"Let him talk." Florian offered her a handkerchief.

"Ian has been dealing in stolen art for years. When he had a buyer, my job was to authenticate the piece he was peddling."

"I take it Ian is the one whose brains you were banging out on the floor in the hotel."

"Right. Ian Hardwicke. We were at school together. I thought the first time I met him that he was the most dashing, best dressed, smoothest fellow I'd ever seen." He paused a moment. "I still think that, I suppose. At any rate, he sort of took me under his wing and taught me about drawing rooms and mindless chatter, how to select clothes and what to drink. Looking back, I suppose it was a lark for him to be tutoring a dolt from a fishing village in the west. I learned about art on my own. It's irony. Ian had no interest whatever in art during our student days. I may be responsible, inadvertently, for giving him the idea that there was money to be made in the field.

"After we graduated he went into importing and exporting. So far as I know, legitimate in the beginning, antiques and art works mostly. I actually don't know how he first got onto stolen pieces. My first was a La Tour he asked me to authenticate. I'm not sure I knew it was stolen. Perhaps if I did, I had managed to forget. It was real, I was pretty certain, though that was not my period. It was all very casual and there was no mention of money, although he did ask me to join him for a long weekend in Paris. At his expense."

Henry walked over to Kim and placed a hand on her shoulder. "I'm sorry, but you have to know."

"Get on with it," Florian said.

"There were half a dozen or so over the years that I verified. There may well have been others I did not know about. This treasure from the museum in Dublin was by far the most daring. And dangerous."

"My God, don't tell me *you* lifted it from the museum."

"No, no. That was done by Calcularius."

"The magician?" Kim couldn't believe it.

"Yes." He turned to Gibson. "He was a sleight-of-hand artist with a police record. Ian caught him a while ago stealing his watch and held it over him so he could use him for odd jobs. The payoff for Calcularius, real name Danny O'Rahilly, the fellow found dead in a Dublin alley the other night, in addition to money, was forged papers so he could come to this country.

"I don't know the details, but somehow Danny dropped the plaster figure he was to use to replace the real thing and running down the stairs, he pushed a guard and the chap fell and was killed. Ian thought it was too dangerous to have him around so he killed him. He didn't tell me that, but I knew when I saw the newspaper.

"The problem was getting the figure into the United States. He asked Sydney to get Kim to bring it but Sydney thought Kim would see it as smuggling."

"Did Sydney know it was stolen?" Did she want to hear the answer?

"No, Ian convinced her it was a replica he needed to get to a collector here for his wife's birthday. He wrapped the figure just like your shepherdess and Sydney agreed to switch the packages, thinking she'd tease you about doing a little smuggling once it was all over. I don't know how Walter got the package. Do you?"

"No." She shook her head. "He was on the plane and asked me to come up to first class and have a drink, and while he was going to ask someone to get our drinks, I saw the picture on the front page of the paper and realized I was carrying the stolen treasure."

"I'm guessing Sydney somehow brought Walter into the loop," Henry speculated. "But when you finally reached your hotel here in New York you had the Meissen again?"

"Right. Walter knocked on the door and said he had the figure and it was safe but I was in danger. By that time Ian was there trying to get the figure. When Walter knocked, Ian put a gun to my head and whispered that I should be quiet. Walter kicked the door in and Ian shot him."

"So the stiff on the floor was Walter. Walter who?"

"Carrasco."

"Who was he?"

"A friend of Sydney's."

"Was he with you in London?"

"No. He took us to lunch in Dublin."

"What does he do? Did he do?"

Kim hesitated. "Sydney said he was a gangster."

"What the fuck? A gangster!"

"But she may have been teasing me. He was handsome and sweet and didn't seem like a gangster."

"You say he told you the figure was safe. Any clue as to where it might be?" Florian asked.

"No."

He looked at Henry.

Henry shrugged

"You're right. I'll have to arrest you. First, I'll read you your rights."

So fast that if Henry had not seen a lot of American television he wouldn't have been able to follow the message.

"Will you be willing to testify against Hardwicke when the time comes? Wait, you'd better not answer that."

"Is this Sydney Reardon?"

"Yes," Sydney answered and waited.

"Florian Gibson. New York Police Department. I'm sorry to bother you in the hospital. I hope you're feeling better."

"Not great, but they tell me that I will in time. They tell me I should be thankful just to be alive. I know your name. Tad has told me about you. How did you get in on all this?"

"Tad called me because Kim was in trouble."

"Is she all right?"

"Yes. She's had quite an adventure. All sorts of problems along the way. She's a little bruised and shaken, but she's fine. I won't spoil her story. She'll want to tell you the whole thing. I've been talking with her and Henry James. May I ask you a few questions?"

"Why not. I've answered questions for the London police. And those who came over from Dublin. Why not talk to New York? You're sure Kim is all right? Is Walter?"

"No. Walter is dead. I hear he's a friend of yours."

"Oh Jesus!" She took a deep breath. "Yes. He was." There was a long pause.

"Want to tell me any more? Kim says he was a gangster. But she also says he didn't seem like one. You may have been teasing."

"No. I wasn't teasing."

"Can you tell me who he worked for?"

"Why not? The London police know. And the ones in Dublin. I'm sure you'll be talking with them. They've been watching him on a whole other matter."

Florian Gibson whistled when he heard the name. "Big time."

"Big time."

"Carrasco knocked on Kim's door and said the figure was safe but she was in danger. Hardwicke was in the room with a gun to her head and when

Walter kicked the door open, Hardwicke shot him."

"Poor Walter. And poor Kim. Imagine living as dangerously as he did and getting shot over what I thought amounted to a joke."

"How did Walter get the figure? Kim thought she had it until she opened the package in her hotel room here."

"After Kim was on the airplane, I was standing in line at a ticket counter and I heard on the radio a report of a stolen object that sounded familiar. I rushed and bought a paper and there it was on the front page. I was frantically trying to figure out what to do when Walter appeared, heading for the plane. I persuaded him to switch packages en route, telling him it was a joke on Kim. Knowing my predilection for practical jokes and sharing the sin he, of course, agreed. It was horrible of me but I thought there'd be no problem.

"If I'm completely honest, my reasoning was that if there *was* a problem he'd be better able to handle it than Kim.

"Obviously I knew then that Ian was involved and I called him as soon as I reached London. No answer, but shortly he came to my flat. I expect Henry has told you what happened next."

"Right."

"Where is Ian?"

"In custody. Any idea where the stolen figure might be?"

"Not really. Perhaps he gave it to The Boss, as he always called him. If he did, you'll never see it. If he didn't do that, I have a hunch his mother has it."

"His mother? Christ, don't tell me she has underworld ties."

"No. She loved Walter. He was a very good son and she thought a very good man. His death must have been a terrible shock. It will be a blow to her if she learns the truth about his career. She believes The Boss is a business man with international holdings and that Walter was becoming increasingly successful under his tutelage. He had a fierce attachment to his mother and if he wanted something to be safe until he figured out what to do, I'd wager he left it with her."

"How do I find her?"

"On Carmine Street. I don't remember the number and I somehow didn't think to bring my address book to the hospital."

"No matter. We'll find her."

"Yes. Please. Be gentle. To her he was a sweet boy. As a matter of fact, he was to me, too."

"It's funny. I'm a cop and my mamma would have thought I'd done something bad the minute the police came to the door. This was a professional bad guy and his mother's sure he's good. Doesn't make sense, somehow. Thanks for your help. I'll let you know what we find."

 It had taken only one telephone call to get the address. He had said he was her son and wanted to be sure the address was correct on her voter registration. He spelled the name and waited while the clerk searched for it on the computer.

"Yes, here it is."

"Carmine Street," Gibson supplied and the woman read the number before he could say anything else.

Her building looked like all the others on the block. She was on the first floor.

"In a minute." He could hear slow footsteps as she approached. "Yes?"

"Good morning, Missus Carrasco. I'm Florian Gibson, New York Police Department." He held out his ID. "May I come in?"

She nodded and held the door open. For a woman whose son was allegedly a gangster, she showed no emotion at the sight of a police caller. But if Sydney was right, she didn't know his profession.

The blinds were partially closed and the room was cool and quiet. The furnishings and carpet were good quality. The upholstered furniture was carefully slipcovered and there were crocheted doilies protecting the arms and backs. Every wall was crowded with family photographs. In a corner of the living room was a round table which held dozens of figurines.

"I'm very sorry about your son."

"Sit down, please." She motioned to a chair and sat facing him. Tears rolled down her cheeks and she made no move to either hide them or brush them away. It was a long time before she spoke. "He was such a good son. I was having coffee. Will you have some with me?"

They sat in the dimly lit room sipping the hot liquid while she talked about her husband, dead many years and buried in Italy. And about Walter.

"He was so good," she repeated. "He paid for this place. Bought everything for me. He always brought presents. All of these. I call them my pretties." She waved a hand toward the table. "The one he brought back his last trip was not as nice. It was little and green and looked old." She had moved over to the table and picked up a small figurine. "I found it in his coat pocket after he was killed. I'll always love it. It's much prettier since I painted it gold."

Florian Gibson thought that after more than thirty years as a cop, nothing could take him by surprise.

He was wrong.

"Son-of-a-bitch," he muttered under his breath. "It is unusual and very pretty," he said aloud.

He didn't have to ask about the object. He didn't have to tell her why he had come. It made perfect sense to her that the big Black policeman had admired her Walter and had come to pay his respects.

Florian walked slowly to the car, jingling his keys. He liked her. He had been gentle as Sydney had asked. He had found the figure. Let the boys from Dublin come and take it from her. They were in for a shock. As he climbed into the car and fastened his seat belt, he began to chuckle. After all the dangerous jokes the others had tried, Walter's mother had the last laugh.

AFTERWORD

It has now been two years since that morning in July when the newspapers predicted the end of the London drought.

Ian Hardwicke is settled in a smart apartment on the Upper East Side of New York City while his clever and expensive lawyers tangle the legal system. Self-defense, he claims for killing Walter. The chap kicked in the door. "If one must kill," he adds, "it was probably wiser in the States to shoot someone with underworld ties."

"Are you an electronics expert or a computer whiz?" one of his attorneys asked. "No one has figured out how that object was removed unless the security system was inactive."

Ian's startling blue eyes peering from an aristocratic face sparkled.

"No, my friend, but I am an expert on human nature. If you couple gullibility with greed you have remarkable success.

"I took the curator's name from a museum directory and made an appointment. He was impressed by my engraved card indicating that I was Francis Falwell, a dealer in eighteenth century art. I explained that I was moving soon to Dublin. I was, of course, concerned about security and had heard that their system was exemplary.

"He was delighted to introduce me to his security officer and explain the system.

"Three visits later the security man and I were chums. I told him I had a wager with the curator that involved having the security system inoperative for one minute—only sixty seconds. I gave him the hour and the date and a few hundred pounds for his trouble.

"You may be certain that after the removal of such an important object during the minute he will never utter a word."

The lawyer shook his head. "Clever." It did not seem expedient to remind his client that after his distracting diversions in New York are exhausted, he still faces charges of murder and theft of a National Treasure in Dublin and attempted murder in London.

Sydney limps slightly when the weather is really damp and cold, but her recovery is remarkable. She is still that American decorator everyone is talking about in London. Her life is filled with concerts, late dinners, laughing too much, drinking too much, as always, but somehow it isn't as much fun. She is haunted by the remembrance that Walter Carrasco is dead because of her predilection for levity.

Kim is sharing a small flat with Henry not far from Trinity and is an understudy at the Abbey Theatre. In fact, she went on for the first time just last week. She is no longer confused and frightened. She is certain that her future is linked with Henry's.

Henry spent eleven months in prison as an accomplice to theft. He is on probation for five years and cannot leave Ireland. He did indeed get the piece to hang together and is now polishing a final draft of a definitive work on Bosch. He is in love with Kim and knows he has been since that first night riding back to town when he wanted her so desperately.

Walter's mother had the last laugh but Walter, who loved a joke, was not around to enjoy it. However, The Boss paid for her to take her son to lie in a plot near his father overlooking the Bay of Naples. She always knew, as Sydney did, that she was the only woman he gave a damn about. She is repaying his loyalty by visiting his grave every morning.

The man called Calcularius was buried in a pauper's grave. Kim couldn't get that frightened, rain-streaked face out of her mind and with Henry she spent many weekends trying to find out more about him. They have recently had his body moved to a village in the west. The marker reads:

Danny O'Rahilly
Conjurer, Actor, Mime
Also called Calcularius

No one in the village could remember him for sure, but there are plenty of O'Rahillys there and at least he has a decent resting place. It is some comfort.

Sydney suggested that they place a replica of the little green man on his grave. "No, let's not," she added quickly. "We've had quite enough jokes."

The little green man?

After extensive and expensive restoration, the figure is once again on a pedestal alone in a dimly-lit room, honored as the most important piece in the collection.

Oh, Florian Gibson. He took early retirement and is now a protective agent. "Who'd have thought I'd end up as a bodyguard? But, Christ," he adds, "who'd have known there was so much money to be made protecting people from their enemies—and their families and friends."